"You are wrong about me, Signor Conte."

Suzanne shook her head at him. "I am not rich."

"No?" He raised a mocking eyebrow. "Then you, too, want money—and a man with a title. My, you are ambitious."

"And you, conte, are rude and overbearing. Why should I think someone as plain as I could possibly interest you? I wouldn't aspire to be a contessa."

He smiled, briefly. "I wasn't talking about marriage. You would not need to be my wife; the position of my mistress would entitle you to everything you want."

Suzanne faced him angrily. "Would it surprise you to know that you don't interest me in the slightest?"

"Would you like me to prove otherwise?" the conte asked, dangerously soft as two strong hands pulled her relentlessly toward him...

Other titles by

CAROLE MORTIMER
IN HARLEQUIN PRESENTS

CAROLE MORTIMER

tempted by desire

Harlequin Books

TORONTO·LONDON·NEW YORK·AMSTERDAM
SYDNEY·HAMBURG·PARIS·STOCKHOLM

For John and Jasper

———————————————————

Harlequin Presents edition published November 1979
ISBN 0-373-70823-8

Original hardcover edition published in 1979
by Mills & Boon Limited

CHAPTER ONE

'Do stand up straight, Suzanne!' snapped Celeste, herself coolly and sophisticatedly beautiful in a green halter-necked sun-dress, a perfect foil for her shoulder-length auburn hair. The two of them had just entered the hotel lounge, its quiet luxury exactly to Celeste's liking. This holiday was costing enough, so why not expect and receive the best? She looked critically at her stepdaughter. 'And do take that expression off your face!'

Suzanne looked at her with wide green eyes. 'What expression?' she asked innocently.

'What expression!' Celeste scoffed cruelly. 'The one of self-pity you've been sporting all week. You look like a lamb for the slaughter. Anyone would think it was you who had to marry an old man simply for his money.'

Suzanne cringed at the crudeness of her stepmother's words. 'Neither of us needs to marry anyone!' she objected. 'It's just you!'

'I don't intend to live in poverty for the rest of my life.' Celeste's blue eyes flashed dangerously. 'If that father of yours hadn't wasted and frittered away all his money, none——'

'Now that's enough!' Suzanne's words came out in an angry whisper. Celeste had picked the unlikeliest places to have an argument, the lounge of one of the most exclusive hotels in London! But it *had* to be exclusive. How else could Celeste meet this ageing millionaire of hers? Suzanne stood her ground, her eyes silently saying she would go no further. 'My father spent what little money he possessed on *you*. And this is how you repay him, with recriminations and scorn.

What he ever saw in you I'll never know.'

She knew she had gone too far by the two bright spots of colour that appeared in Celeste's usually creamy cheeks whenever she was about to forget she was supposed to be a lady. Her manicured and lacquered nails clenched into fists, and if she had been a child, Suzanne would have said the other woman was about to have a tantrum. As it was, she was probably about to make a scene.

'All right, Celeste,' she sighed deeply. 'I'm sorry for that remark. Put it down to the fact that I'm tired and we've been in each other's company constantly for six days. We probably need a break from each other.'

Celeste wasn't so easily mollified. 'Tired!' she burst out. 'What on earth have you to feel tired about? Oh, I agree with you about the company—I'm getting sick and tired of looking at you if the truth be known. But you have no reason to feel *tired*, living here in the lap of luxury, your every whim arranged with ease. Tired!' she repeated in disgust.

Suzanne looked about the room self-consciously, aware that they were causing quite a lot of eyes to be turned in their direction. Although their words couldn't be heard, Celeste's stance was obviously one of anger and her own one of obstinacy. 'We'll continue this conversation some other time, Celeste,' she said stiffly. 'I'm going to my room, but you go ahead and have your afternoon tea as planned.'

'Well, thank you! I'm so glad I have your permission,' Celeste said sneeringly.

'Oh, I've had enough!' Suzanne turned on her heel and left the lounge, walking uncaringly to the lift that stood empty. The other two lifts seemed to be either going up or down already, and although it seemed rather selfish to take the lift up to the sixth floor just for herself, she didn't feel like waiting for one of the others to arrive.

Celeste was daily becoming more and more impossible. She wouldn't mind if she had wanted to come on this visit to London with her stepmother, but she hadn't. Oh, the lure of luxury for a few weeks had been all too tempting, but the thought of sharing the so far unseen sights of London with Celeste of all people had rather put the damper on her enthusiasm. And so far Celeste had proved just as unreasonable as she had thought she would be. Celeste hated sightseeing, in fact, the hotel and the pool were Celeste's only haunts, and Suzanne had perforce to share them.

God, it was so restricting! She wanted to explore the depths of the town, wanted to walk about London until she knew every inch of it. Maybe that would be a bit impossible, she had heard that even some Londoners could become lost in the more densely populated areas, each street looking like the last. But that had been the reason behind her coming here with Celeste, the reason she had told her friends that the idea sounded so appealing.

Robert, especially, had been against the idea of at least six weeks' separation, but Suzanne had thought this perhaps another thing in London's favour. Robert was all right as a friend, but what had started out as a mild flirtation was deepening into something more serious on his side. But it certainly wasn't on hers. Robert was fun and he made her laugh a lot with his crazy ideas, but surely there had to be more to love than making her laugh. What had happened to the romantic, passionate side of a relationship? Robert's kisses certainly did no more for her than anything else she would enjoy in an apathetic sort of way. There were certainly no flashing lights and sounds of thunder when they kissed, just a warm pleasant feeling, the same as she might feel after an enjoyable evening or meal.

But then according to Celeste the flashing lights

and thunder were purely a figment of the romantic's imagination. Romantic rubbish she called it, and so far Suzanne had to agree with her.

Once in her room she threw down her sun-glasses and magazine, running on to the balcony and looking longingly at the sun. It was all right coming to her room to escape Celeste's temper, but by doing so she had also denied herself the freedom of the pool. She was in London wasn't she! One of the most exciting cities in the world! So where was her excitement? She looked down at the teeming streets below her. Somewhere down there could be the man of her dreams, the man who would let her see the flashing lights and hear the thunder.

He would be dark, of course, she had always preferred men with dark colouring, and he would have beautiful dark teasing eyes. And tall—he would have to be tall. At just over five feet herself she felt cosseted and cared for in the company of tall men. Yes, she knew exactly what he would look like: tall, elegant, with a lithe masculine body. And he would look at her as if she were the most beautiful thing in his world.

She burst out laughing at her thoughts. Now she was just being imaginative. Beautiful was something she wasn't and never could be. Short bouncing blonde curls surrounding a heart-shaped elfin face could never be called beautiful in any language. As far as she was concerned, her only redeeming feature was her huge green almond-shaped eyes surrounded by thick naturally dark lashes. But what man would want to marry her for her eyes? Robert would! But in no way could he be made to fit into her picture of her ideal man, with his reddish-brown hair and laughing blue eyes. And he wasn't tall, at least, only moderately so, and his physique could only be described as thin. No, she would have to face it and so would Robert, he just wasn't the man for her. Besides, he wasn't nearly sophisticated enough. Her ideal man was older than herself by at least five years, worldly and knowledgeable, with all the self-assurance she herself lacked.

She sighed deeply. What was the use of dreaming, with someone like Celeste about she didn't stand a chance with any man, let alone one of good looks. Celeste, with her tall proud body, her thick vibrant auburn hair, and most of all her perfect beautiful face. Suzanne's father hadn't been the first man to fall for Celeste's deceptive innocently charming demeanour. He had been flattered and bemused by the evident interest of such a beautiful twenty-two-year-old to his already forty years. So flattered that within a few short weeks of meeting the two of them had become man and wife.

And a few weeks after that Suzanne had been sent away to school! She saw her father occasionally during the school holidays, although more often than not she had been told she was to stay on at school for the holidays too. Not that she had minded too much at first, a lot of other girls did it too, but after a time it had begun to pall. The few times she did go home for the holidays Celeste was noticeable by her absence. Not that Suzanne minded this either, she much preferred to be alone with her father, but it was apparent that her father would much rather have been with his young, not always faithful wife.

She had naturally been upset when her father was killed in a road accident not long before she was due to leave school. She had been sixteen, and it had been then that she had found that although her father had lived his life to the full in the last six years, he had done it by using up every penny he possessed. Celeste and she had been left destitute, and although it was a blow to her, it was complete devastation to Celeste. None of her so-called friends, male or female, had

wanted to know her then, making it perfectly obvious
that if she couldn't pay her way then she wasn't welcome. Most of these people had been hangers on anyway, and now there was nothing to hang on to.

For Suzanne the future had been clear. She was
to go to college and later to university, her main sub-
jects being anatomy and physiology, which she hoped
eventually to go on to teach. But for Celeste things
hadn't been so easy, if missing meals and walking everywhere could ever be called easy. How Celeste had survived the next three years Suzanne hadn't gone into
too deeply, but she felt sure it must have involved a
man with money. Now Celeste had decided she wanted
more than money. She wanted marriage, and if possible, a title. This hotel dealt only with the élite and
titled, and as Suzanne knew, Celeste was a very determined woman. But as she had tried to point out, most
of the earls or whatever they were called were as broke
as they were. But Celeste wouldn't be daunted, she felt
confident enough of her own beauty and determination
to catch herself a rich prize.

No one had been more surprised than Suzanne when
her stepmother had invited her to stay here too, and no
one but a fool would have turned it down. She had lived
for too long in a badly decorated bed-sitting room, missing too many meals than was good for her, and studying much too hard to turn down the opportunity of six
weeks of absolute luxury. She hadn't enquired where
the money had come from for them to book into one
of the most exclusive hotels in London, and any guilt
she might have felt about Celeste paying all the bills
was quickly quenched. Celeste had calmly informed
her that she was only required to lend respectability to
her own stay there. Escorting her stepdaughter for her
health was the story Celeste had put about, and
Suzanne's too thin, delicate appearance lent truth to
such a lie. Never mind that her experiences of the last

three years had given her a toughness and strength of body and mind that made her a much more durable person than Celeste. At least, she hoped it did.

Celeste's constant truculence was beginning to be an irritant she was finding it impossible to bear. She had imagined Celeste would quickly find her doting rich suitor and leave her pretty much to herself. Not so. Celeste was very choosy about her escorts, and although Suzanne knew a couple of them were rich and very interested in her stepmother, Celeste quickly spurned them. It was as if she were waiting for something—or someone. Someone in particular.

Oh, it was too nice a day to let Celeste spoil it for her! She would go down to the pool anyway. She quickly changed into a green bikini that matched her eyes and slipping on a beach robe of the same colour to cover her near-nakedness she ran quickly out of the room and into the lift.

The clothes had been Celeste's idea too, insisting that her denims and tee-shirts weren't suitable attire. Not that she was supposed to look too attractive, just elegant enough to be thought the stepdaughter of a rich widow. Another of Celeste's lies. If it was known she was using every penny she possessed on this last fling then she would be known for what she was, a gold-digger.

At almost five o'clock in the evening the pool and its surrounding loungers were beginning to empty. Most of these people would shower and rest before changing for dinner, then spend an hour or so drinking, and the same after their meal. Suzanne knew the routine so well, and she was sick of it all. Well, tonight she wasn't going to do that. She would laze by the pool for as long as she felt like it, go up and shower and change in her room before strolling over to one of the cafés she had seen in the square and treating herself to a simple meal. She only hoped Celeste didn't bother to look in her room but just went down to dinner without her. Another argument tonight would be more than she could bear.

Slipping off her robe and dropping her sun-glasses on to a lounger, she ran lithely to the edge of the pool to jump capably into the heated blue water. Mmm, it was delicious! She pushed back the hair that had plastered to her face, licking droplets of water from her lips. Over the last few days she had managed to acquire a golden tan and her hair looked very blonde against the darkened skin.

Turning on her back, she swam effortlessly from one end of the pool to the other, revelling in her solitariness. At exclusive places like this hotel there always seemed to be someone standing beside you ready to carry out the least little request, and while it may have seemed rather exciting the first couple of days, this attention soon became rather tedious. But for once the waiters all seemed to be elsewhere, and she relaxed completely, closing her eyes and drifting dreamily.

'Excuse me, *signorina*,' a deep voice broke into her meanderings. 'You are alone here?'

Suzanne trod water, looking to the nearside of the pool. Wow! She blinked rapidly. The man of her dreams! Tall and lithe, dark hair, quizzical teasing eyes, and those faint lines at either side of his nose and mouth giving evidence to his sophistication and experience. He looked anything between thirty and thirty-five, much older than the five years' difference she had wanted in their ages, but everything else was perfect. She couldn't take her eyes off him. He was fantastic, marvellous, and she couldn't believe she was seeing him.

'*Signorina?*' He frowned his puzzlement at her long silence, his blatant good looks not marred by the action. He stood at the side of the pool, relaxed and confident, his only attire a pair of white bathing trunks that clung like a second skin and emphasised the darkness of his own skin.

There were many foreign people staying at this hotel and she couldn't help her curiosity at his being sure she was English. 'Why did you address me in English?' she asked him, completely ignoring his own question.

He shrugged his shoulders and smiled, showing clear even white teeth, giving him an oddly boyish look. 'With hair the colour of corn you would most likely be either English or American. You also have their air of freedom.' He indicated the deserted pool area. 'And not many women would brave this isolation with a dangerous Venetian roaming about,' he teased her.

'Oh, you're a Venetian!' she sighed ecstatically. He was absolutely perfect. In every way.

He bowed politely, and while it might have appeared effeminate on any other man dressed informally as he was, on this man it appeared only as a charming gesture. 'Vidal Martino at your service, *signorina*.'

She climbed breathlessly out of the pool, dropping her proffered hand self-consciously as she realised it was dripping water everywhere. 'Suzanne Hammond,' she supplied shyly.

'I am honoured to meet you. Are you alone here?' he repeated his first question.

'I'm alone here at the pool, but not at the hotel. My stepmother is probably in the process of changing for dinner right now.'

Vidal Martino smiled again, looking deeply into her wide green eyes. 'The proverbial wicked stepmother?'

Suzanne laughed. 'Not really, although we aren't the best of friends either.' She picked up her towel and began to dry her wet curls. She must look an absolute mess! Whatever must Mr Martino think of her?

He indicated that she sit on a lounger, only relaxing the long length of his own body on to the one next to her after she had complied. 'I arrived only this afternoon. You will have to excuse my curiosity concerning yourself. You live with your stepmother?'

'Oh, no,' she shook her head emphatically. 'No, I'm merely holidaying with Celeste. Since my father died three years ago Celeste and I haven't been the best of correspondents,' she laughed nervously. 'I'm sorry, I didn't mean to bore you with my family history.'

'And you have not done so. I was merely curious as to why one so young as yourself should be staying at such a staid respectable hotel. I would have thought one of the more modern hotels, with dancing and music, would have been more to your liking.'

'But surely the same applies to you, *signore*?'

Vidal Martino shrugged his powerful shoulders. 'As I am a Martino it is expected of me to stay here.' He grimaced his distaste. 'I am here for one night only. I have just arrived from the Palazzo Martino, which is just as respectable, let me assure you.'

'A *palazzo*!' She reassessed her new companion. 'You surely aren't a count or something, are you?' It would be just her luck if he was. No one of such importance would be interested in ordinary Suzanne Hammond. Unless of course he was one of those impoverished counts that seemed to exist in abundance? She looked at him sharply—no, this man certainly wasn't impoverished. There was arrogance and bearing in every line of his superb body.

He laughed with genuine amusement. 'Not I, Signorina Hammond. Unlike you, I am not so lucky as you seem to be with your stepmother. I have the proverbial wicked step*brother*, the Conte Cesare Martino. And I would like it very much if I had no correspondence with him for three years.' The last was said with bitterness and the boyish charm left his face.

'You don't like your brother?'

'Cesare is difficult to like or dislike. He is like a rock, and you cannot feel emotion for a rock.' He sprang up from the lounger. 'It is too depressing to talk of Cesare. Would you like to go for another swim?'

Suzanne was still muddling over Vidal Martino's remarks concerning his brother. So his brother was a count! A much older, embittered man, by the sound of it, who tried to rule this charming man with an iron will. She couldn't imagine anyone more charming than Vidal Martino, so she could only assume that the Conte Cesare Martino was unreasonable to his fun-loving younger brother.

She shook her head regretfully, looking at the watch she was just attaching to her slim wrist. 'I really must shower and then find myself some dinner.'

Vidal Martino put a restraining hand on her arm, and Suzanne found she liked that warm caressing touch, feeling strangely bereft as his hand was removed. 'You do not intend dining at the hotel?'

'Not this evening. I feel in need of a change of scenery. I thought this evening I might try one of the little restaurants just outside the hotel. They look nice, and more my—my taste, if you know what I mean?'

'Oh, I know exactly what you mean,' he smiled at her. 'Would it be permissible for me to join you? I too feel in need of more simple surroundings.'

She was taken aback by his request. Surely he had something better to do than join her, people he should go and see if he had just arrived? It would appear not, by the look on his face.

'Signorina Hammond?'

'Oh, yes, Mr Martino, of course you can join me if you want to. I'm not going anywhere exciting, though.'

'Believe me, I have had enough excitement these last few weeks to welcome a quiet dinner with a beautiful companion. Venice can be rather exhausting.'

'Surely no more so than London.'

'Perhaps not,' he conceded. 'If you intend either

working or enjoying the night life. Unfortunately I did both.'

'You—you work?' Although his athletic body and active brain did not point to him spending his time idly, neither did he look the sort of man who sat behind a desk all day.

Vidal Martino laughed aloud, a deep pleasant sound that evoked a smile on her own face. 'Cesare would say not, but I would say yes. My brother has many business interests all over the world. I run the London office. Again Cesare would say it runs itself, but ultimately I have to make the final decisions—and face Cesare if anything goes wrong.'

'You actually live in England?' Excitement entered her voice as she thought of the possibility of seeing this man when she left the hotel. She mentally shook herself. She was just being silly. Just because he was at a loose end this evening it didn't mean she would ever see him again. But she wanted to! Oh, yes, she wanted to.

'For perhaps six months of the year.' A look of consternation crossed his face. 'I will have to be excused dinner, I am afraid. I have just remembered a previous engagement that I cannot break. Meeting you put all other thoughts out of my mind. Could I join you for drinks later this evening?'

'You don't have to meet me at all, if you don't want to. I won't be upset.' But she would, she would! Vidal Martino was her ideal and she couldn't lose him so soon after meeting him.

For answer he took one of her hands firmly in his own, threading their fingers together intimately. 'That is a great pity, because I personally would be very upset—*upset*?' he repeated with disgust. 'I would be devastated, Suzanne Hammond. My engagement this evening is one that I cannot evade, otherwise I would do so. But please do me the honour of meeting me later. I should return by ten o'clock, ten-thirty at the latest. Is that too late for you?'

'Oh, no, no, of course not. I rarely retire before midnight.'

'Then I am permitted to join you in the lounge later?'

'Please,' she smiled at him shyly, acutely aware of her hand still held firmly in his. It seemed incredible that she had only met him an hour earlier, and even more incredible that he actually wanted to see her again. Her hand was suddenly free and he ran to the edge of the pool, diving into the clear depths with hardly a ripple. He struck out with strong movements, swimming two lengths before coming back to the side of the pool.

'I will see you later, Signorina Hammond—Suzanne,' he amended warmly.

'Very well—Vidal,' she replied breathlessly, surprised at her own daring.

With a last intimate smile Vidal Martino sank beneath the water. Suzanne picked up her wrap and towel and walked dreamily back into the hotel. Having dinner anywhere else didn't seem such a good idea now, not if there was a chance of seeing Vidal later in the evening. There was always the possibility that he might return early.

It was already seven o'clock by the time she reached her room, and seven-fifteen by the time she had showered. Choosing what to wear was a difficult decision. Should she wear the clinging black silk and look sophisticated, or wear the lemon chiffon that made her hair look like spun gold? She finally decided on the black silk. At nineteen to Vidal Martino's thirty-two, thirty-three, she wanted to appear as worldly as possible.

Her hair was another problem, a golden mass of riotous curls, it was difficult to tame to any semblance

of order. Pinning the majority of the curls on to the top
of her head, she allowed one or two tendrils to curl
provocatively at her temples and three or four at her
slender nape. It gave her a look of childish sophistication and she knew it was as good as she was going to get.
A light make-up and pale lipstick to add colour to her
face and she was ready to face even the watchful
Celeste.

A hasty look in the mirror showed her that she had
what Robert would call her 'adult look'. Robert! She
had completely forgotten him since her meeting with
Vidal Martino. As she had thought, Robert paled to
insignificance when compared with her ideal man. And
since meeting the vibrant masculine man in the flesh,
Robert had been put completely out of her thoughts.

Her hotel room door swung open without any warning and she didn't need two guesses who it was, in fact,
she didn't even need to turn round. Nevertheless she
did turn round, only to come under the scornful gaze
of Celeste.

'Well, well, well,' she drawled silkily, swaying gracefully into the room to walk mockingly round Suzanne
as she willed herself not to be bothered by Celeste's
taunting. 'And who is this little lot for?' she flicked one
of the curls caressing Suzanne's temple.

Suzanne flinched away from her stepmother. 'What's
what little lot for?' she asked steadily.

'Why, the outfit, darling,' purred Celeste. 'Do you
have an assignation with one of the waiters? Carlo perhaps?'

'Don't be childish,' she snapped, picking up her
evening bag in preparation to leave the room. 'I'm
merely dressed for dinner, nothing more.'

'Really?' I haven't noticed such an effort on any
other of the evenings we've been down to dinner.'

'Are you trying to tell me I usually look a mess?'

'Of course not, Suzanne. I would have told you so if you did. So who is it for?'

'No one,' Suzanne said sulkily. 'I just felt like making an effort. Do you object?'

'Oh, no.' Celeste shook her head, her vibrant auburn hair gleaming as she moved. 'I just hope you aren't getting any big ideas about your own future. I made it obvious to you before we came here that it was my fortune we were seeking. Have you forgotten?'

'How can I forget anything so disgusting?'

'Quite,' Celeste's mouth twisted sneeringly. 'And I think it's just arrived.'

'Really?'

'Yes, really. You don't have to sound quite so eager to get rid of me.' Celeste looked at her stepdaughter suspiciously, picking up bottles at random from the dressing-table to study their contents.

Suzanne saw her mistake as she felt Celeste's keen looks in her direction. It was just that it would be so convenient if she didn't have Celeste watching her every move over the next few days. But she mustn't let Celeste know that; already she had given away too much to this perceptive woman.

'Come along, Suzanne, we can discuss this better over dinner. Well, perhaps not better, but at least in comfort.'

'All right,' agreed Suzanne, herself eager to get dinner over with as soon as possible. The sooner she had eaten the sooner she could go to the lounge and wait for Vidal.

Dinner was delicious as usual and Celeste in her more mellowed mood was quite convivial company. They even laughed together a couple of times, something they had never done before. Celeste often laughed *at* Suzanne but never *with* her.

'You many not believe this, Suzanne,' Celeste said quietly as they drank their coffee at the end of the meal. 'No, I'm sure you won't believe it. But in my own selfish way I loved your father very much.'

'You can safely say that now, can't you, now that he's dead and can't refute such a statement?' Suzanne said vehemently.

'Are you trying to say I didn't make your father happy?' Celeste gave a slight smile. 'I don't think you can say that with any degree of honesty.'

'Maybe not. But I was his daughter, didn't I deserve to be included in his life too?'

'I said in my own selfish way, Suzanne, and that didn't include you. Children have never entered into my plans for my future, and that means other people's as well as my own.'

'Surely this wealthy man will want children?' Suzanne pointed out spitefully. Celeste certainly brought out the worst in her.

'Perhaps. It may be a necessary evil,' she said in a bored voice. 'Perhaps just one, to satisfy the man's vanity.'

Suzanne looked about her curiously. The only man she could see who remotely fitted into Celeste's mercenary plans was a man sitting at a corner table of the dining-room, but even he didn't have to be the man, this dining-room was open to the public and he could just be a visitor, not an actual guest. He was a man in his mid-sixties, with grey streaked hair and a body that was running to fat. He was quite handsome for a man of his obvious years, but surely Celeste couldn't be contemplating marriage to a man so much her senior.

But why not? Suzanne's father had been eighteen years her senior, so what did it matter that this man could give her at least thirty years? It didn't matter in the slightest to Suzanne, Celeste must make her own future, in any way she wanted. But to marry a man like that! It made her feel slightly sick.

She looked at her stepmother. Celeste might be hard

and grasping, but surely she deserved something better than that. Her father *had* loved the woman, so she couldn't be all bad. But she couldn't be all good either, not when she could shut out a child of ten from her own father's love.

'What on earth is the matter now?' Celeste asked impatiently. 'Surely I haven't shocked your puritan little mind again? Dear, oh dear, Suzanne, you'll have to toughen up if you want to survive in this harsh cruel world your father and mother introduced you to. It's a rough world out there and you have to be the same if you want to survive, and I intend to do just that.'

'I'm not shocked, Celeste,' Suzanne gave a rueful smile. 'I think I'm past that where you're concerned.'

Celeste laughed, a completely natural gesture that added to her already considerable beauty. Blue, often mercenary eyes were filled with amusement and Suzanne wished that Celeste would act this naturally all the time. How much more attractive it made her. Not that her stepmother needed any extra attraction tonight, dressed as she was in a clinging russet-coloured gown that should have clashed with her rich auburn hair, but somehow didn't.

'Why were you looking so serious, then?'

Suzanne shrugged, unwilling to start another argument. 'I was—I was just looking round to see if I could spot the man—you know, the man you——' she broke off in embarrassed confusion.

'The man I've picked out to be my husband,' finished Celeste, completely unembarrassed herself. 'And who did you decide it was?'

'Well, I——' Suzanne looked at the elderly man she had picked out earlier and Celeste followed her gaze.

'Not him, Suzanne!' she burst out laughing. 'Give me credit for a little taste!'

'Then who?'

'Oh, he isn't here, darling,' again Celeste affected

that false drawl. 'He's otherwise engaged this evening, but I'm meeting him tomorrow. He's absolutely fascinating, Suzanne, a shame he's only a means to an end.'

'So who is he, Celeste? Don't keep me in suspense!'

'You are interested, aren't you? Well, I suppose it makes a change from your apathy. His name is Vidal Martino.'

CHAPTER TWO

'VIDAL MARTINO?' Suzanne echoed weakly.

'Mmm—lovely name, isn't it? And so is the man. I think Celeste Martino sounds quite distinctive, don't you?'

Suzanne felt physically sick. Oh, God! Not Vidal Martino! Why couldn't it be anyone else but him? And Celeste had said she was meeting him tomorrow. Oh, how could he, when he had already arranged to meet *her* this evening! Her distress must have shown on her face, because Celeste looked quite concerned.

'Are you all right, Suzanne?' She touched her arm. 'You've gone terribly pale.'

'Oh, I—I'm fine. I felt rather faint for a moment, but I'm all right now,' Suzanne lied. How could she feel fine when she was dying inside? In the space of an hour she had fallen in love for the first time in her life, and now it was completely shattered by a few short words. Celeste meant to marry Vidal Martino, and knowing Celeste that was exactly what she would do.

'It is rather warm in here,' Celeste agreed. 'Why don't you go out into the garden for a while?'

'Yes. Yes!' Suzanne said jerkily, rising unsteadily to her feet. 'It is rather stuffy, isn't it? I won't be long.'

Celeste sat back lazily. 'Take your time, darling. I may just wait here on the offchance that Vidal returns earlier than expected.'

'Oh, oh, I see,' Suzanne said dully. She had to escape from here, be on her own for a while to sort out her thoughts.

The garden was definitely cooler than the hotel dining-room, although the hotel was air-conditioned. The fragrance of the many flowers out here was exquisite. She had escaped here many times during the last few days, when she couldn't stand Celeste's over-bearing attitude any longer. And now this! For the first time in her life she had found someone she was sure she could love, and he was destined for Celeste! She was certainly no competition for the beautiful red-head, and she might as well give up any hope of keep-ing a man like Vidal Martino interested in someone as plain as herself when Celeste wanted him.

It was a bitter blow and one she had faced once be-fore in her life—and both of them dealt by Celeste. First her father and now Vidal Martino. She should hate Celeste, but she didn't. At times Celeste showed a gentler side of her character, a facet of her nature she took great pains to hide. And she mostly succeeded.

She said Vidal had arranged to meet her tomorrow —he couldn't have wasted much time after leaving Suzanne this afternoon. This knowledge hurt her some-how, and she wasn't feeling particularly friendly to-wards him when she saw him walking across the garden towards her.

'Suzanne,' he put out his hands to her, drawing her close to him. 'You were not waiting in the lounge,' he scolded gently. 'Luckily I spotted your hair in the darkness.'

'I see,' she said huskily, unable to draw her gaze away from those warm compelling brown eyes. 'My step-mother was in the lounge.'

'Ah, I see,' he nodded understandingly. 'You did not want to meet me in front of her. Well, I think she must have gone to bed because the lounge was deserted when I came through just now.'

Suzanne felt angry at his casual dismissal of Celeste, and yet excited too. Celeste hadn't made such a big impression on Vidal that he didn't want to see *her* again. 'Oh,' she licked her lips nervously. 'Did you— Did you have a nice evening?'

Vidal Martino grimaced. 'As pleasant as one could when visiting a grandmother. When Cesare's mother married our father her mother moved in too. She now lives in her own home in England and complains that we neglect her. She does not think that it would have been better for all of us if she had stayed at the Palazzo like any other grandmother would. And of course Cesare visits her regularly when he is here.' Again that harshness entered his voice when talking of his brother. 'But I must not bore you with my family. Shall we go in and have that drink now?'

Why not? Celeste wasn't in the lounge, and by the look of things she would have to make the most of this meeting with Vidal Martino, tomorrow Celeste would take over. She nodded her head, renewed eagerness entering her eyes. 'I'd love to.'

He grinned at her. 'Good.'

As he had said, the lounge was deserted, and within minutes they were ensconced at a corner table with two drinks on the table in front of them.

'So,' Vidal turned on the bench seat they were both sitting on, his knee touching hers intimately before it was politely withdrawn. But he was still sitting very close to her and she found she liked his closeness, liked the fresh male tangy smell that his body exuded and the expensive aftershave that she had come to realise he wore exclusively. 'Tell me a little about yourself, Suzanne.'

'There isn't much to tell, and I'm not being trite when I say that, there really isn't much to tell. I'm a student, training to be a teacher, eventually.'

'If the job is available,' he put it mildly. 'There seems to be an abundance of unemployed teachers in this country at the moment. I can sympathise with you.'

'Mm, it could all be wasted effort when I've finished.'

'And do you live on your own?' He offered her a cigarette, lighting one for himself at her refusal.

'In a bed-sitting room? I certainly hope so, there's hardly room for me, let alone anyone else.'

'And you have a boy-friend?'

She looked at him sharply, but could see only mild curiosity in his clear brown eyes. 'I have male friends,' she said carefully. 'But none that I feel serious about.'

'But one who feels that way about you,' he guessed shrewdly. 'If he feels this way why has he allowed you to come to London without him?'

'I don't feel that way about him, it's as simple as that.'

'It is a good enough reason—and I for one am glad of it. I would not like to think I was—cutting in is, I believe, the right expression.'

Suzanne laughed. 'Mmm, but you aren't—or at least, you wouldn't be if you intended——' she broke off confusedly.

His dark brows lowered with concern. 'My age worries you, perhaps?'

She looked startled. It certainly wasn't his age she was worried about, it was Celeste, beautiful Celeste with her lethal charm. She shook her head wordlessly.

'I am thirty-two. Is that much older than you?'

Suzanne had to laugh at his earnestness. As if a little thing like age mattered where someone of his looks and charm was involved. 'You shouldn't ask a lady her age, Vidal,' she rebuked him teasingly.

His dark eyes twinkled back at her. 'I know, but you are not a lady—I mean, you aren't——Oh, dear, I am wording this badly. My English is not as fluent as I would wish it to be. What I meant was that you are a beautiful young girl and have no reason to hide your age.'

'You had me worried for a moment.' She couldn't hold back a grin. Wow! When he smiled at her like that ...! 'I'm nineteen—just,' she supplied.

'You have been on your own since you were sixteen?'

'Just about. But I was on my own long before that really. Daddy and my stepmother lived out of the country most of the time, and so I was left in boarding school.'

'At least I cannot say that. Cesare always cared for me when I was a child. I was fifteen when our father died and Cesare was forced to take up the responsibilities of being the head of the family. I am afraid I was not always a well-behaved child, far from it in fact.'

'I can believe it.' And she could too. He still had the look of an impish child when he teased her and she felt sure the Conte Cesare Martino must have had his patience sorely tried. 'And how did his wife feel about that.'

This question seemed to cause him a certain amount of amusement, and Suzanne could only wonder why. Until he told her. 'Cesare is not married. Many have tried and many have failed, but as I have told you, it is hard to love a rock, and believe me, Cesare is pure granite. One day I think a woman will come along and knock him completely off balance. It must be so, I am sure of it. He is a Venetian, and we are a warm passionate race. Cesare cannot be so different,' he smiled with relish. 'I hope I am around when it happens, I think I would like to see him bowed by love for a woman.'

'That isn't a very nice thing to say,' she scolded.

'You are right, but I find I have many of these thoughts about my austere brother. You would know why if you were ever to meet him.'

Suzanne gave a little laugh, a soft gentle sound that riveted her companion's eyes on her glowing face. 'I don't think there's any chance of that!'

The smile faded from her face as she saw the scowl on Vidal Martino's face, and following his gaze she saw the reason why. A man had just entered the lounge, a tall aristocratic man with a dark look of disapproval in his rigidly held features. Suzanne was instantly aware of his air of arrogance and she wasn't surprised when the manager of the hotel began bowing subserviently to him, only to be waved imperiously away again. Icy grey eyes settled on the two of them sitting in the corner of the room and Suzanne felt herself stiffen as the newcomer strode towards them with long easy strides.

'You are about to be proved wrong,' muttered Vidal, rising slowly to his feet.

Suzanne's startled gaze swung to the man now standing beside their table, her eyes widening with shock. Surely this couldn't be the Conte Cesare Martino! This man was too young and he didn't fit her picture of him at all. That over-long blond almost silver-coloured hair, and those steel grey eyes couldn't possibly belong to a Venetian. And yet his skin was a dark swarthy colour. The whole effect was very startling and very attractive, much too attractive for any woman's peace of mind.

'Cesare,' Vidal Martino said firmly, confirming Suzanne's suspicions. 'I did not expect to see you tonight.'

The Conte's eyes flickered momentarily over Suzanne as she remained seated, and if anything his look became even more contemptuous. 'So it would appear,' he said coldly, his voice only slightly accented, much less so than his brother's, a deep slightly husky sound that commanded attention.

'And what do you mean by that?' Vidal's face became flushed with anger.

Suzanne compared the two men and could find little resemblance, except perhaps in their physique. Both looked powerful men, although she would hazard a guess that any battle these two entered opposed to each other, be it verbal or physical, the Conte would always emerge the winner. As brothers, half-brothers, they bore no resemblance to each other. One was so dark in colouring, and the other so fair and yet with that dark contrasting skin. There couldn't be more than six or seven years difference in their ages and yet the Conte had such a distinguished air that he appeared older. And no wonder, if he had had to take over his duties as the Conte Martino at such an early age.

'I merely meant that as you are already occupied then of course you could not have been expecting me,' the Conte answered his brother's rather heated question. 'Are you not going to introduce us, Vidal?' As he said this the Conte lowered his tall frame to sit on the other side of Suzanne, and Vidal had perforce to join them.

'Suzanne, my brother the Conte Cesare Martino,' he gave in sulkily. Suzanne was again reminded of a little boy and her resentment towards his brother grew for interrupting what should have been a perfect evening spent with Vidal. 'Cesare, this is Signorina Hammond, Signorina Suzanne Hammond.'

She felt her hand taken into a firm grip and at last looked up as the Conte's silver-blond head neared her hand, kissing her suddenly warm flesh with those cold firm impassioned lips. Grey eyes widened slightly as they met the sparkle in her green ones and Suzanne felt strangely unreal for a moment before he calmly broke that gaze.

'*Signorina* Hammond?' he queried softly.

'Yes,' she replied breathlessly, feeling curiously as if she had run for miles and miles and now felt winded.

'I only ask because I was informed that a *Signora* Hammond was staying here.'

'That would be Suzanne's stepmother,' Vidal put in resentfully. 'And what, may I ask, have you been doing this evening, Cesare?'

'The same as you, no doubt, visiting my stubborn and wilful grandmother. When she informed me of your visit to her I thought it only polite to see you before I retired. As you only arrived this afternoon I thought perhaps you would be alone. I can see I have wasted my time.' Again those grey eyes flickered over Suzanne's still form.

Usually rudeness didn't bother her, but she was perfectly well aware that coming from this arrogant man it was a gross insult. He certainly wouldn't talk about one of his own countrywomen with such ill-disguised contempt, and definitely not in front of them. 'If you are referring to me, *signore*, then you are quite wrong. I'm not detaining your brother,' she said icily.

'Whether you are or whether you are not is not Cesare's concern,' Vidal cut in. 'I am no longer a child, Cesare, but a grown man. You would do well to remember it.'

The Conte stood up in unhurried movements. 'And you would have done well to remember, Vidal, that the Grant contract was an important part of my plan for greater expansion into America,' the words rang out with contempt. 'And if you had contacted me immediately on your arrival this afternoon instead of— instead of flirting with this child—we may have still been able to salvage something from the mess. As it is, Leroy Grant has cancelled any further business with us.' He bowed stiffly to Suzanne. 'Miss Hammond. I will see you in your office tomorrow, Vidal.'

There was no mistaking the anger in his voice and Suzanne watched him nervously as he walked out of the lounge. The hand that lifted her glass shook with delayed reaction and she sipped the fiery liquid gratefully. So that was the Conte Martino! Vidal was right, that man was pure granite. She looked at Vidal and was shocked by his appearance. His face was paled somewhat and he was glaring after the Conte with undisguised dislike.

She put out her hand and touched his arm tentatively. 'Vidal?' she said questioningly. 'You mustn't .

let his anger bother you so much. I'm sure he'll have forgotten it by tomorrow.'

Vidal seemed to visibly drag his attention back to her, smiling slightly at her concerned face. He patted her hand reassuringly. 'Cesare forgets nothing. But I am unconcerned with his anger. Grant had already decided not to sell to us before we even made our offer. It was his rudeness to you that I find unforgivable. And do not say it does not matter, because I can see it did. He annoyed and upset you.'

'Perhaps,' Suzanne admitted. 'At the time. But it isn't important, at least, not important enough to ruin our evening.'

'To me it is. He would not have spoken to one of our own nationality in that way. Cesare dislikes the free-dom of your countrywomen.'

'I had already guessed as much,' she said with a light laugh. 'But it doesn't matter. He wasn't half as old as I imagined him to be.'

Vidal Martino studied her suspiciously. 'You do not find him attractive, do you?' he demanded haughtily, looking curiously like his brother at that moment.

'Why, I——! No, of course not. What a strange thing to say!'

'Not so strange when you consider what he has—money, harsh good looks, and most important of all, a title. I am not so foolish that I do not realise how at-tractive these things can be to a woman. Cesare is thirty-seven, only five years my senior, and yet at times he reduces me to a mere schoolboy. Imagine what havoc he could evoke in a babe like yourself.'

'I don't need to imagine anything, I've seen him with my own eyes, and as you've already said, he only an-noyed and upset me. What do you take me for, Vidal? A gold-digger?' Her green eyes sparkled angrily.

Vidal gave a throaty chuckle. 'Forgive me, Suzanne. Of course I think no such thing. You must try to understand. Cesare has always taken everything he wanted, and occasionally it has been women whom I thought I had prior claim to.'

These words gave Suzanne a warm glowing feeling and yet she still felt angry. 'Now you're being silly. You heard what your brother called me, a child. He obviously disliked me.'

'Perhaps, perhaps not. It does not matter, as long as you disliked him.'

'Well, I did,' she said impatiently. 'And I think this conversation is all rather pointless. You will be going to your apartment tomorrow and I'll probably never see you again.' She badly wanted to see him again, but in the last few minutes she had learnt that you could not go on looks alone. Vidal Martino might be perfect to look at, but his jealousy of his brother over even the little things certainly wasn't an endearing quality. But perhaps he had good reason to feel that way—who was she to judge?

'You will most certainly see me again, Suzanne,' he said softly, caressingly, and Suzanne felt her bones melt at the warmth in his eyes. 'We will meet often. You are staying long in London?'

Suzanne shrugged. 'Until Celeste says we leave.'

'I see. Then I could perhaps call on you some time during the next few days? I am unsure of when it will be,' he grimaced. 'Cesare will make sure I make reparation for losing the Grant contract, so I will probably be kept busy.'

'I wouldn't like to cause any more trouble between the Conte and yourself,' Suzanne said stiffly.

Deep brown eyes looked at her imploringly. 'Please do not be angry, *cara*. I would like very much to see you again. Answer truthfully, would you like to see me also?'

'Well, yes, but I——'

'Then it is settled.'

Suzanne would have liked to point out that he might find it quite difficult meeting Celeste and herself without Celeste actually finding out about it, because it was a sure fact that her stepmother didn't intend sharing Vidal with anyone. But the temptation to see this fascinating man again was too much for her. Why should she care about the Conte's disapproval if Vidal didn't? And it was only when reminded of his brother that Vidal became not quite the man of her dreams, and she doubted very much if she would ever meet the Conte again. She nodded her head wordlessly.

Vidal grinned. 'Good. Would you care for a short walk in the garden? It is still quite warm and the perfume delightful.'

She knew that if she went out into the garden with him he was bound to kiss her goodnight, and her senses jumped in anticipation. Why not? This was London, sin city some people called it, so why not accept a kiss from a romantic Venetian? She smiled at him shyly. 'I would love to.'

The garden seemed more than usually beautiful and Suzanne walked with this tall Venetian as if in a hazy dream. Everywhere appeared to have a special look and the flowers a strong heady perfume, and she knew this was entirely due to the presence of Vidal Martino. Never before had she felt so breathlessly nervous, as if she were floating on a silver cloud. This had to be love, this wild beating of her heart and the excitement of her senses by just being with him. What on earth would happen to her when he kissed her! She felt as if she would faint from pure delight at being in his arms.

'You have beautiful hair, Suzanne,' Vidal said close against her ear, making her aware of just how close to her he was. A slight movement and his hard thighs came close against the back of her legs and she knew he was standing directly behind her. Her breath caught and held in her throat and she felt afraid to turn around in case she broke the spell. She could feel his soft warm breath on the nape of her neck and she waited expectantly for his next move.

Strong hands closed firmly around the top of her arms and she was turned slowly to face him. His dark head bent and his lips lightly caressed the hollow visible at the base of her throat. Suzanne quivered with pleasure and sighed her disappointment as those firm passionate lips were reluctantly removed. She could see his handsome features in the moonlight and her heart turned over just at the sight of him.

'You are trembling, Suzanne,' he said, huskily soft. 'Do I frighten you?'

She shook her head. 'No.'

'Ah,' he smiled gently. 'Then dare I hope that I— excite you?'

Suzanne blushed a fiery red. 'Vidal!' she said reprovingly.

'Now I have shocked you. It is not shameful to admit to physical pleasure. With you I feel this pleasure. There, you see, I am not ashamed to admit such feelings.'

'But you're a man!'

'And it is only men who are permitted to feel like this? Come, Suzanne, your studies must have told you differently.'

'I'm not such an innocent, it's just that it isn't something one usually discusses.'

'But why not? Sometimes the discussion can be almost as pleasurable as the action. But I will not tease you any more, no matter how delightful you look when you blush. Don't ever lose that innocence,' he said, suddenly serious. 'It is a fascinating part of your charm.'

'I have to become a woman some time, Vidal,' she pointed out, her cheeks still aflame with colour. No

Englishman would ever talk in this way—well, not on such short acquaintance anyway.

'To become a woman does not necessarily mean you lose your innocent approach to life. You are youthful and refreshing and it would be a great loss for you to become hardened and sophisticated.'

Suzanne could quite well believe this was the type of woman he usually entertained; wasn't Celeste such a woman? 'Thank you,' she smiled shyly. 'I think that's the nicest compliment I've ever had.'

Dark velvet eyes held her mesmerised and she waited expectantly while his dark head bent slowly for his lips to claim her own. Strong arms held her against the lean length of him and her own arms slowly slid up his shoulders and around the back of his neck to lengthen and deepen the kiss. At first his lips played gently with hers until finally he parted the softness of her mouth to greater explore her sweetness.

Never before had Suzanne experienced such a caress. It was beautifully sweet while being temptingly serious. And yet she felt disappointment too. No flashing lights and sounds of thunder to tell her this was the man she could love, and yet his kiss gave her more pleasure than she had felt before with any man. But no flashing lights and sounds of thunder! This knowledge spoilt everything. Was she to believe Celeste and admit that these things just didn't happen? It would appear so, because she felt sure she was falling in love with Vidal Martino.

She felt bereft when at last those lips were removed but sighed with pleasure as he moved to continue his exploration of her creamy throat and shoulders. 'Vidal!' She couldn't suppress her groan of pleasure at his touch.

'You are beautiful, Suzanne, so beautiful.' He drew back regretfully. 'But for now we must part. I will call you and arrange a meeting. You will come?'

Her eyes glowed and her lips throbbed and it was all she could do to nod her agreement. A fleeting touch of lips and Vidal was leading her back into the hotel. They parted at the lift doors with a formal goodnight and at Suzanne's surprised expression Vidal looked pointedly at the hotel receptionist, who was watching them with unconcealed curiosity.

'I have no intention of giving them a free show,' he told her with a smile, keeping his voice low and only for her ears.

Suzanne saw that the hotel porter was also watching them and she felt rather resentful at their intrusion into her perfect evening. But of course it hadn't been perfect! Hadn't the Conte Cesare Martino seen to that? Oh well, the latter part had more than made up for it. 'Goodnight, Vidal,' she said huskily. 'I'll look forward to hearing from you.'

The intimate glow in his eyes was his only indication that he would have liked to do more than politely kiss the back of her hand. Blushing prettily, she gave him one last glowing smile before pressing the button to close the lift doors. She hugged herself tightly. Wasn't he wonderful, perfect, all that she had ever wanted in a man! And yet still the nagging doubt remained. No flashing lights and sounds of thunder. She dismissed this as unimportant, it had to be. Celeste must be right, because this had to be love she felt. It had to be!

She walked dreamily into her room, discarding her evening bag and her shoes before looking at her reflection in the mirror. She didn't look any different, a little starry-eyed perhaps, but that was all. Shouldn't there be something more than that to show how gloriously happy she felt, something more tangible than this bubbling feeling inside?

The door flew open without warning and Celeste marched purposefully into the room, interrupting and breaking into Suzanne's dream world. 'What a liar you are, Suzanne!' she spat out with a sneer. She looked about the room as if she were surprised to see Suzanne alone. 'Where is he, then? Skulking in the bathroom?'

'Where is who?' Suzanne's eyes were bewildered. 'What are you talking about, Celeste? Who could possibly be in my room at this time of night?'

Celeste gave a harsh laugh. 'Don't act the innocent with me, Suzanne. Not any more. I saw you—I saw you, I tell you! Out there in the garden!'

Suzanne began to look apprehensive. 'You—You saw me?' Oh, God, no! Celeste would never forgive her.

Celeste walked about the hotel room, a mocking smile marring her beauty. 'Mmm. Mooning about the garden with your gigolo.'

'Gigolo?'

'Yes, gigolo. He could hardly be anything else, he thinks you're rich, remember? I was right, wasn't I? It *was* Carlo. How could you do it, Suzanne!' She sat down on the bed. 'You know my position here. You know how important it is that we retain an air of respectability. The Martino family won't stand for any scandal. If it's known that my stepdaughter keeps company with the waiters then the respectable appearance we've built up here will become non-existent. How could you do it, Suzanne? How could you!'

Suzanne felt a glimmer of hope. Celeste didn't realise that her companion in the garden had been Vidal Martino, and she certainly wasn't going to tell her. 'You believe I was with Carlo?'

Her stepmother shrugged. 'What does it matter which one of the waiters it was? You may go out with anyone you choose when at home in Manchester, but not here. I won't allow it. If Vidal Martino gets to hear of this affair you'll ruin my chances.'

'V-Vidal Martino?' Suzanne echoed hollowly. How

could he not hear of it when it had been him all the time?

'Yes, Vidal Martino!' Celeste stood up angrily. 'So this little flirtation must stop. Do you understand?'

'Celeste, you can't——'

'I can, Suzanne! This affair stops or you'll return to that hovel you call home immediately. I mean it, Suzanne,' she walked to the door. 'So you'd better tell your little friend that it's over.'

Suzanne stared at the closed door. Well! Just who did Celeste think she was? How dared she walk in here and proceed to order her life? The fact that Celeste considered her to have been meeting a waiter and not Vidal made no difference. She had no right to come in here and issue orders concerning Suzanne's conduct. No right at all.

She walked restlessly about the room. Celeste must have seen her from the window of her own hotel room, they both had that view from their window. Obviously the darkness had prevented her from recognising Vidal, but her own golden hair must have shown up very clearly in the moonlight. Thank God she hadn't actually seen the person who was with her; there was no telling what she would have done if she had known that.

Suzanne was late down to breakfast the next morning. She had tossed and turned most of the night. She was feeling so indignantly angry that she had great trouble getting to sleep at all. Celeste's reprimand had stayed in her thoughts late into the night until finally she fell into a restless sleep.

Celeste was just finishing her coffee when Suzanne arrived at their table. She looked at her stepdaughter critically. 'That's a pretty dress,' she remarked coolly.

Suzanne sat down reluctantly; she had hoped Celeste

would already have breakfasted. 'You've seen it before. You paid for it.'

'There's no need to be bitchy, Suzanne. I only said what I did last night for your own good. My marriage will benefit you as much as it does me.'

'Why?' Suzanne asked sharply. 'Because I'll get you out of my life once more? You don't know how much I wish for that, Celeste. If I'd realised just how obnoxious you were going to be I wouldn't have agreed to come here at all. I've managed without you so far and I'll do so again.' She poured herself a cup of coffee. 'I can't wait for the day.'

'No one forced you to come here, Suzanne. Luxury appealed to you, didn't it?'

'Yes, it did, I don't mind admitting it. But I wish now that I hadn't bothered—I can't stand being here with you.'

'Now that's a shame, because I quite like you. You're like your father in many ways.'

'Will you leave my father out of this!' Suzanne's cup clattered down into the saucer. 'I couldn't give a damn what you do with your life, but leave my father out of it.'

'All right, Suzanne, I will. We never liked each other, did we? Perhaps you were right and I shouldn't have shut you out of our life together. We would maybe have been friends then. Well, it's too late now,' she crumpled her napkin and stood up. 'I'll be seeing Vidal this morning, so you please yourself what you do.'

'Thanks.' Suzanne obstinately kept her eyes downwards, helping herself to a piece of toast and concentrating on spreading it with butter. 'I was going to anyway.'

Celeste laughed, looking beautiful and vital in a black and white spotted sun-dress. 'That's what I thought. I may be out all day, so it's up to you what you do. As long as you don't meet that waiter,' she added darkly.

'I'll meet who I please, *when* I please,' Suzanne looked at her defiantly. Celeste's casual mentioning of her expected meeting with Vidal only made her feel more angry and contemptuous. How could Vidal help but find the attractive and sophisticated Celeste more beautiful than she?

'Not on my money you won't,' was Celeste's parting shot.

Suzanne suddenly wasn't hungry. Her appetite hadn't been too great to start with, but now it was non-existent. She left the dining-room to collect her bathing things and then went to the pool, intending to spend the morning lazing beside the pool and bathing in the soothing water.

Carlo, the waiter, brought her out a long cool lime juice at her request, placing it on the low table beside her. 'Miss Hammond,' he began nervously. 'Someone is asking for you in reception, someone of importance,' he indicated her bikini. 'It would not be proper to meet him dressed so.'

Suzanne's eyes opened wide at Carlo's tone of rebuke. It wasn't usual for the staff at this expensive hotel to act in this way. Perhaps Carlo guessed that she wasn't one of its rich patrons, but a masquerader. But even so ... 'Who is it, Carlo?' she asked sharply, not a snob herself, but she didn't welcome this boy's familiarity either.

Carlo, one of the Italian staff at the hotel, broke into a spate of his own language, the pure complicated Italian that only they could speak. Suzanne understood little of it, although she knew a little of the language, once having shared a flat with a young Italian girl over here for her education. The only thing that seemed to make any sense out of this tirade was the name Martino. Suzanne sat up, her eyes bright and happy. She had seen Vidal Martino leave the hotel with Celeste earlier, but perhaps he had returned to see her.

'Mr Martino?' she said excitedly. 'Is Mr Martino waiting for me in reception?'

'*Sì, sì*,' Carlo nodded vigorously, watching as Suzanne jumped to her feet, pulling on her bathing robe. 'But, Miss Hammond, it——'

Suzanne didn't wait to hear any more but ran into the hotel, slowing down to a fast walk as she neared the reception area. Her face glowed and her eyes shone. Vidal had come back to see her, she felt sure of it. She knew he had checked out of the hotel at eleven o'clock, she had seen him leave, and she had also seen Celeste clinging to his arm. But he had come back to see *her*.

She looked around for him excitedly, coming to a shocked halt as she saw who *was* waiting for her. 'Conte Martino!' She said breathlessly.

CHAPTER THREE

HE walked towards her with those familiar long easy strides, completely male and dominant. He took her proffered hand, bowing low over her slender fingers. 'Miss Hammond.' Those icy grey eyes searched her startled face. Her hand was slowly released and he stepped back away from her. 'You did not expect me,' he surmised correctly. 'Did the waiter not explain that I wished to see you?'

To see her! But why? Last night he had treated her with nothing but contempt, so what did he want with her now—not more insults, surely? 'I—I thought you were——' She broke off in confusion. It sounded rude to say she had thought him to be someone else, even if it was true. She shook her head wordlessly.

'You thought I was Vidal,' he guessed correctly again. 'But did the waiter not explain that it was *Cesare* Martino, and not Vidal?'

Suzanne put up a nervous hand to her disordered hair. It badly needed washing after her dip in the pool and at the moment surrounded her heart-shaped face in riotous curls. Oh, why hadn't she stayed to listen to the end of Carlo's conversation, for she felt sure now that he had been going to explain exactly who her visitor was. 'He may have done,' she said hurriedly, realising he was looking at her strangely for her prolonged silence. 'He was talking in Italian at a very fast rate,' she explained. 'I'm all right with bookish Italian if it's spoken very slowly, but anything else defeats me, I'm afraid.'

'But surely he must have known this,' the Conte said harshly. 'All the non-English staff are requested to speak only English.'

'Oh please, don't be angry, Mr—Signor Conte,' she amended hastily. 'He was so excited, because you're a count, I suppose, he just forgot for a moment.' She looked down at her lack of clothing. 'That's probably the reason he told me I wasn't dressed properly too,' she said wryly.

The Conte's swarthy face darkened with anger. 'He dared to do that?' he demanded coldly. 'A waiter told a guest at my hotel that she was insufficiently dressed? But this cannot be!'

Only one thing made any sense to Suzanne. '*Your* hotel, Conte Martino? You *own* this hotel?'

'That is correct. And many more like it throughout Europe and America. Sadly not enough in America— that was why the Grant contract was so important to me. But no matter, I did not come here to discuss business. In fact I came here to apologise for my behaviour yesterday evening. I may have been annoyed with Vidal, but my behaviour towards you was unforgivable.'

'You don't have to apologise to me,' Suzanne said quickly. 'I quite understand.'

Quite frankly she felt bewildered. Conte Martino actually owned this hotel she and Celeste were staying at. Had Celeste known this when she had decided to come to London, to this particular hotel? Suddenly she felt sure that she had. That was the reason Celeste had seemed as if she were waiting for something or someone—she had been. She must have guessed that sooner or later Vidal Martino would be a guest here at his family's hotel, or perhaps she hadn't needed to guess at all, perhaps she had known. Perhaps she knew more about the Martino family than Suzanne realised. But if this were so, then she must also realise there was a *Conte* Martino, a man with good looks, money, and most of all, a title. So why was she seemingly interested in *Vidal* Martino? It was all a mystery to Suzanne, a complete mystery.

'So,' he broke effectively into her thoughts, 'is my apology accepted?'

'Of course, Conte. But there was no need, really.'

He looked about the lounge, finally indicating for her to sit down in one of the luxurious armchairs provided. As she sat down she became blushingly aware of her lack of clothing. A thigh-length bathing robe was hardly suitable attire to entertain a real live Conte in. She should have listened to Carlo! He could have delayed the Conte while she ran upstairs to her room to change. Oh well, it was too late now.

'I do not agree,' he said haughtily. 'I am not usually so abrupt to visitors at my hotel. You have visited London before?' he asked suddenly, those strange grey eyes intent upon her.

'No.' What else could she say?

'You like it?'

'I haven't actually seen much of it,' she told him almost guiltily.

'You have not been in London long?'

'A week,' she admitted reluctantly, feeling almost as if she had committed a sin; the way the Conte was looking at her she could almost believe she had. Goodness, a *Conte*, a Venetian aristocrat! And he was every inch that, from his styled curiously light hair to his immaculate linen and hand-made leather shoes.

'I see,' those firm well-shaped lips pressed together disapprovingly. 'I naturally assumed you to be a tourist.'

'Oh, I am. It isn't that I don't want to look around London,' she said hurriedly. 'I would really love to. Unfortunately my stepmother doesn't like sightseeing. She finds it boring.'

'And you feel obliged to keep her company?'

Suzanne laughed, a lighthearted youthful sound that

made those grey eyes narrow even more. 'Heavens, no!' she shook her head. 'Celeste doesn't need me. Not now anyway, not when she has——' she broke off, realising she couldn't actually say *that* to this man; Vidal was his brother. Anyway, she shouldn't talk about such things to a stranger. But what a handsome stranger, handsome and intriguing. He raised a dark eyebrow at her sudden halt, strangely dark brows in comparison with that silver-blond hair.

'Yes?' that clipped voice enquired.

She shrugged. 'It isn't important. But I should be free to see some of London during the next few days. I'm really looking forward to it.'

'Then you will do me the honour of letting me be your guide. There are many places not to be missed by any tourist.' He looked enquiringly at her startled face. 'There are many places of interest among the surrounding shops and restaurants that do not jar on the nerves. I cannot believe that you have been in London a week and not been to see these things.'

'But I have, Conte. But I promise to see them all now, it's what I'm here for, after all. Celeste, my stepmother, will probably be entertained elsewhere during the next few days, so I'll be able to go sightseeing to my heart's content.'

That arrogant face tightened, the nostrils flaring out on that haughty nose. 'You refuse my invitation to show you London?'

Suzanne looked at him searchingly, her green eyes shadowed. She fussed nervously with her sun-glasses in her hand and seeing his eyes on her movements stopped abruptly. 'I didn't say that, Conte. I believed your offer merely to be one of politeness.'

'It was not.'

'But I—I hardly know you. I can't ask a complete stran——'

'But I am not a stranger. We were formally introduced yesterday evening, otherwise I would not be here now. Vidal introduced us and so everything is perfectly in order. Do I take it that you still refuse my offer? I assure you it was made only out of a desire to show you your beautiful city. But if the brother of Vidal is not good enough for you——'

'Conte Martino!' Suzanne was really shocked now. 'I didn't say anything of the sort. You are the Conte Martino, and I would never do or say anything to imply that I felt anything but respect for you. As for Vidal, well . . .' she raised her hands helplessly, 'I met him for the first time yesterday too.'

If she had expected to shock this haughty man then she was mistaken; not a flicker of emotion showed in those pale grey eyes. 'You met here at the hotel?'

'Yes, at the pool.'

His look encompassed her scanty attire. 'Which is where you were today, until a few moments ago. You did not know Vidal before this?'

'As I said, *signore*, I met him for the first time yesterday.' Was it really such a short time ago? It seemed much longer.

'You seemed rather—friendly when I arrived.'

'Possibly,' Suzanne said stiffly. Really! This man looked down his arrogant nose far too much for her liking! 'Your brother is an easy person to talk to,' she said defiantly.

'I have no doubt,' his mouth twisted with bitter humour. 'You know that Vidal is betrothed?'

'B-betrothed?' A betrothal in Venice was almost as binding as a marriage, that much she had learnt from her flatmate.

'I see you did not know. Vidal perhaps did not feel obliged to mention this fact because it has not yet been made official. An understanding between the two families for many years, you understand. It is to be announced during his next time at home with us.' He straightened one snowy white cuff beneath the cream linen of his lightweight suit.

'Why are you telling me this?'

He shrugged those broad powerful shoulders. 'I thought it might perhaps have been of interest to you.'

Suzanne's green eyes became stormy and she gathered up her purse and sun-glasses in readiness of leaving. 'You thought no such thing, *signore*,' she said with suppressed anger. 'And you certainly didn't come here out of politeness,' she gave a harsh laugh. 'That was the last thought on your mind!'

Grey eyes became flinty with displeasure and at any other time she would probably have run away to hide. But not today. The Conte Cesare Martino had been nothing but condescending and downright rude to her since the first time he had spoken to her, and she had no intention of giving him the satisfaction of seeing her cower as she felt sure many other people had done before this superior man.

The Conte looked self-assured and completely unruffled by her outburst. Except for those eyes, icy grey eyes that could look right through you. 'Then just what would you say my purpose was in coming here?' he asked coolly.

'To warn me off Vidal,' Suzanne answered unhesitantly.

'You are presumptuous, Miss Hammond!' he said in that stilted voice.

She shook her head. 'Not at all, Conte. Though why I should present a threat to your barbaric plans for your brother I have no idea.'

His mouth twisted mockingly at her anger. 'And what *barbaric* plans would these be?'

Suzanne shrugged. 'An arranged marriage.' It surely had to be that if Vidal could behave with her as he had yesterday. And he certainly hadn't seemed in a

hurry to talk lovingly about a fiancée. In fact, he had
seemed reluctant to talk about his personal life at all,
and no wonder, with such a powerful man trying to
pressurise him into marriage.

The Conte flexed his long legs before standing up,
towering over her as she also scrambled to her feet.
Goodness, he was tall! 'Our ways are not yours, Miss
Hammond.'

'They certainly aren't!' How arrogant he was! 'Am
I to take it your offer to take me sightseeing is now
rescinded?' A devil inside her seemed to force her to
taunt him in this way. He was so powerful, so self-
confident, and seemed to consider himself omnipotent.

His look could only be called glacial. 'My offer stands.
Am *I* to take it you are now transferring your undoubt-
able charms to me? Is Vidal to be cast aside in favour
of a better prospect?'

Suzanne's blood boiled. Only this man could have
turned the tables so neatly on her for her barbed taunt.
'Certainly not!' she said indignantly. 'I can hardly re-
place Vidal when he hasn't been mine to start with.
And you wouldn't be a likely candidate under any circumstances.'

'You mean a Conte is not up to your standard?'

There was no missing the sarcasm in his voice. Her
eyes narrowed. 'Just what do you mean this time?'

The Conte bowed formally. 'Forgive me. I was under
the impression that it was myself and not Vidal who
held your interest.'

'How conceited you are!'

'Not at all. I am well aware of the power of money,
and the receptionist informed me yesterday evening
that you had asked of my whereabouts almost every day
you have been here. I naturally assumed that you were
using Vidal as a means to an introduction.'

'Oh, naturally,' she said sarcastically. 'It's the sort of
thing I usually do, chase after strange Venetian counts

and when thwarted resort to the younger brother. I do it all the time! If you'll excuse me, Conte Martino, I think I have to go to my room and be ill.'

She didn't wait to see his reaction to this outburst but ran quickly to the stairs leading up to her room on the sixth floor. She negotiated the stairs without thought. How dared he! How dared he come here and try to ruin something that had started off so wonderfully. First Celeste and now him. Why did they have to drag what had seemed like a dreamlike romance down to the everyday basics? First Celeste had supposed it to be a waiter and now that man—*that* man had accused her of being after bigger game, a *conte* no less, and not just any *conte* but himself, the Conte Cesare Martino.

What woman in her right mind would want to chase an arrogant brute of a man like that! The anger started to leave her rigidly held body and she slowed down her pace. It was much too hot to be running about like this, especially up six flights of stairs. And really she could answer her own question. *Any* woman, in her right mind or otherwise, would want such a man. But she certainly hadn't been asking for him at the reception desk. Why, she hadn't even known of his existence until yesterday. Celeste knew more about this family than she ...

Celeste! That was it. It had to be. Hadn't the Conte mistaken her for *Signora* Hammond last night? Celeste was the one who had been asking for him every day. But why? Surely it was *Vidal* Martino she was interested in. Hadn't she said as much when talking about him? Suzanne shook her head dazedly. It was about time she and Celeste had a serious talk about this and not just arguments as they had been doing. It might help her to understand what was going on if she knew Celeste's motives for her actions.

Once in her room she showered and changed into a

pretty pink vest top and white linen skirt. She had smuggled a couple of pairs of her denims into her suitcase, but had soon realised that the rich sophisticated people who frequented this hotel would frown disapprovingly on such attire. Celeste didn't even know she had them with her or they would have been promptly put out for the maids to throw away.

She decided to follow up her idea of yesterday and eat in one of the smaller cafés in town. It didn't look as if Celeste was going to be back for lunch, so she might as well take advantage of this opportunity. With the sun beating down on her and the people around her all looking comparatively relaxed her ill-humour soon left her. She had half expected the Conte to be still in reception when she walked through, but there had been no sign of him.

Suzanne had no idea of the attractive picture she made with the sun giving her hair a golden hue and her eyes glowing with anticipation of her little outing. After days of confinement to the hotel in the company of Celeste this walk in the town was like a breath of fresh air on a spring day. The cafés and restaurants were busy at this time of day and Suzanne walked along until she found one that wasn't quite so crowded, entering the hot but pleasant-smelling restaurant with more confidence than she might have felt in the company of Celeste. Not that Celeste would demean herself by entering one of these quaint home-cooking restaurants. Celeste preferred more sophisticated fare, and the hotel supplied that in plenty.

Since she had not an extensive knowledge of Italian, the menu would have been a complete mystery to her if there hadn't been a short but telling description of the dishes added below each name. Her Italian flatmate, Maria, had introduced her to a few Italian dishes and she finally decided on her favourite spaghetti bolognaise, not very exciting but something she enjoyed

and didn't have too often nowadays. She knew it would
be delicious, and with a creamy coffee would not be too
expensive. Not that Celeste was mean with her money,
but Suzanne didn't want to have to tell her stepmother of her walk and meal out, and if she spent too
much money it would be impossible not to do so.

Her meal was lovely, much the best spaghetti bolognaise she had ever tasted. It had obviously just been
prepared on the premises and was piping hot, besides
having a flavour that was unlike anything she had
ever tasted. Leaving her money for the meal and a
sizeable tip she wandered back out into the sunshine,
deciding to explore some of the streets that branched
off from the main street.

As soon as she moved out of the busy street and down
one of the tiny side-streets the day seemed to become
darker. Buildings stood tall either side of this narrow
road and Suzanne became enthralled with the different
architectures and the other people who were obviously tourists like herself, all enjoying themselves. She
didn't know how far or for how long she had walked,
but suddenly she realised that all the houses looked
the same and she could no longer find her bearings.

Her panic grew as she began to look about frantically
for something she knew, a recognisable face, anything.
People were beginning to look at her strangely and she
stopped an old man, intending to ask the way. 'Please,'
she begged. 'Please, can you help me?'

The man looked at her blankly with bleary eyes before breaking into a string of abuse that was totally in-
comprehensible to Suzanne in her distress. Manchester
was a big city, but it was a city she had lived in most
of her life. Here she knew nothing and no one, and
nothing was in the least familiar. She was lost, completely and utterly lost.

She felt a hand at her elbow and spun round to face
her assailant. The man at her side spoke rapidly to

the old man in sharp English, causing the man to skulk off with a scowl in their direction, mainly directed at Suzanne. And she had only wanted him to help her! Well, she had certainly got help now, only not from someone she relished being beholden to.

The Conte steered her firmly away from the man and back in the opposite direction to the one she had been taking. Suzanne shook off his restraining hand. 'Take your hands off me! What do you think you're doing?'

Dark brows met over those curiously grey eyes and Suzanne longed to ask him the reason for his unusual colouring. 'I thought I was helping a lady in distress,' he bowed distantly. 'It seems I was wrong—on both counts.' He turned on his heel and walked away.

Suzanne ran after him, grasping pleadingly at his arm. 'Oh, please!' she beseeched him. 'I'm sorry, Conte. I didn't mean to be rude, but you frightened me, appearing suddenly like that when I thought I was lost and alone.'

'You should not have wandered so far away from your hotel. You do not know your way about London and you look very suspect, a lone woman wandering around without thought of a chaperone.'

'I don't need a chaperone,' she scoffed. 'I'm old enough to take care of myself.'

'So you have just proved,' the Conte said dryly.

'That was just a chance happening,' she retorted heatedly. 'It could happen to anyone who doesn't know their way about.'

'Exactly.'

Suzanne almost had to run to keep up with his long strides. 'All right,' she sighed. 'I'm sorry. I admit that I didn't know where I was going and I shouldn't have gone off alone like that.'

'No, you should not.'

'How did you know where I was anyway? I didn't see you behind me.'

'You were not intended to. You appear to be a very independent young lady. I felt sure you would not accept advice from me. I spotted you leaving the restaurant as I was on my way to a business meeting. Your hair is unmistakable.'

'So you followed me?' Suzanne looked at him curiously. The arrogant Conte Martino followed a nobody like herself? But why?

He nodded. 'At a distance. I wanted to assure myself you would be all right. You were not.'

Suzanne sighed again. 'I've already said I'm sorry.'

'So you have.' He stopped. 'You are back at your hotel now and I trust you will not roam about on your own again. There are guides at the hotel for just such a reason. You have only to ask.'

She saw that they were indeed back at the hotel. It had taken much less time to get back and she could only wonder at the Conte's intimate knowledge of the streets of London, but perhaps he spent a lot of time here. She smiled at him gratefully. 'Thank you very much, Conte Martino. It was very kind of you to help me.' It was a genuine gesture and yet the words still seemed to stick in her throat.

He smiled at her mockingly. 'Very prettily said. And you will not explore alone again?'

She shook her head, her blonde curls bouncing enticingly. 'Not if you say I'm not to.'

'I do,' he bowed haughtily. 'Goodbye, Miss Hammond.'

'Oh, Conte! I forgot,' she put out her hand to delay him and stopped the movement as she saw the disdainful look on his face. 'It doesn't matter,' she muttered.

'Now you have started you may as well finish,' he advised shortly. 'You should never stop once you have decided to do something.'

'Really? Even if it would be imprudent to continue?'

'And would it be that?'

'Not this time. I merely wanted you to know that it was my stepmother and not I who had been asking for you.'

'I see,' those grey eyes mocked her. 'Thank you for telling me of my—mistake.'

Suzanne's green eyes widened. 'You don't believe me, do you?'

Dark brows rose at her verbal attack. 'Is it important that I should?'

She held herself stiffly. 'It is to me, Conte. Whatever else you may think of me, I am not a liar.'

'Whatever else?' he queried mildly. 'Why should I think anything of you at all. We met for the first time only yesterday.'

'It seems longer,' she returned defiantly. 'Much longer.'

'I am glad I have made such an impression on you.'

'You could hardly do anything else when you literally warned me off Vidal. Tell me, Conte, do you have to do this often?'

She had all his attention now. 'Do what, Miss Hammond?' he asked coolly.

'Warn women off your brother. Does he make a habit of forming unsuitable friendships? Unsuitable in your eyes, I might add.'

'My brother's behaviour, suitable or otherwise, is none of your affair, Miss Hammond. I have told you of Vidal's betrothal, but I can do no more. If you choose to continue seeing him then that is between the two of you.'

'But you disapprove, wholeheartedly.' She spoke the words he was perhaps too polite to say.

He shrugged. 'I can do no other in the circumstances.'

'And what circumstances are they, Conte? Your brother may be betrothed, but that doesn't stop him feeling attracted to other women. After all, he knew about his fiancée, I didn't.'

'I do not care to discuss this any further.'

'I think you're right, Vidal is old enough to make his own decisions.'

'So you intend to continue seeing Vidal,' his eyes were flinty, 'and nothing I say will deter you?'

Suzanne had no intention of continuing to see Vidal Martino, but she wasn't going to tell the Conte that, let him think what he might. She had a healthy respect for marriage, and although Vidal was only engaged she knew that engagements were rarely broken in his country, especially not by the man. If broken at all it had to be broken by the girl, for her own good, and if she wanted another man to offer for her. Besides, she and Vidal had only known each other a day, and although she found him very attractive she didn't want to cause any trouble between Vidal and his family— well, no more than she already had.

'No,' she lied.

'I see.' His gaze raked mercilessly over her slim body and Suzanne moved uncomfortably, unwilling to let him see how he unnerved her.

'What do you see, Conte?'

'A very young girl who defies conventions, who goes after her goal no matter who or what stands in her way, a young girl who wants money and position in life no matter how she gets it. Vidal is rich, I grant you, but I do not intend dying just yet, so the title may never be his. Even then it may pass to my son.'

'So you do intend marrying one day, Conte? I had begun to think that it was only Vidal who had the arranged marriage in your family.'

'My intended bride died.' His words were clipped and stilted. 'Now if you will excuse me I am already late for an appointment.'

Suzanne watched him leave, dismay written all over

her face. The Conte had looked bitter and bleak as he had left, and she was left with the inevitable knowledge that she had caused it. She had believed him to be invincible, but a few short words had penetrated that urbane shell he hid behind.

She entered the hotel slowly, her thoughts still on the Conte. Vidal was the handsomer of the pair, but it was the Conte who was the most striking and stayed in the mind. He was a much deeper personality, unlike Vidal in every way, and yet both were attractive individuals. The Conte would be a hard person to get to know, but once a trusted friend would remain so, Vidal was a more shallow person and yet more easily likeable. But he wasn't for her; the Conte's information had seen to that.

Carlo, the waiter, was crossing reception as she entered the hotel and she smiled at him, and then wished she hadn't as he stopped and came over to her. 'Miss Hammond, I am sorry if you thought me rude this morning. I did not mean to be so.'

'I know that, Carlo,' she accepted easily. 'As soon as I realised who my visitor was I knew you were right about my clothing. It wasn't suitable at all.'

'You were not annoyed at my forwardness?' he asked anxiously.

'I was surprised at first,' she admitted. 'But as I said, once I realised it was the Conte Martino I understood.' She looked at him closely. 'Did the Conte say something to you after I had spoken to him?'

Carlo flushed uncomfortably. 'Signor Conte was not pleased——'

'He *did* say something,' Suzanne said angrily.

'Well ...' Carlo paused. 'This *is* his hotel, *signorina*. And I should not have been familiar with one of the guests.'

Suzanne almost laughed at his grave expression. 'You weren't being familiar, Carlo, you were trying to be helpful. I was just too silly to understand what you meant. I wish I had now, I looked slightly ridiculous clothed like that when the Conte was dressed so formally.'

A ghost of a smile lit his face. 'I am glad you are not angry, Miss Hammond, although the Conte ...'

'Never mind the Conte, Carlo. I made no complaint and I certainly don't intend doing so.' Turning, she saw Celeste entering the hotel, looking beautifully perfect in a lime green silk dress that clung to her tall shapely figure. Her eyes blazed as she saw Carlo standing just behind her stepdaughter, and Suzanne smiled gratefully at the hotel manager as he reached her before the angry Celeste.

'Miss Hammond,' David Brewster smiled stiffly, a tall middle-aged Londoner, who despite his age still managed to be handsome, in a mature sort of way. His hair was iron grey, but this only lent him an air of distinction, and he had all of the pride of the older Londoners. He might only be the manager of this fine hotel, but he certainly seemed to bow to no one, except perhaps the Conte. But she was trying to forget *him*! It wasn't an easy task. 'Miss Hammond, I hope you have accepted Carlo's apology. He's usually a polite boy, hardworking and very helpful to our guests. I can't comprehend his behaviour in this affair. And the Conte a personal friend of yours! It isn't——'

'Oh, but he isn't!' burst out Suzanne, still aware of the approaching Celeste. David Brewster looked at her enquiringly. 'The Conte isn't a friend of mine,' she explained hastily. 'Personal or otherwise.' Really! What on earth had the Conte been saying to these people to give them that impression?

'But the Conte expressed most definitely——'

'Suzanne,' purred Celeste, threading her arm through Suzanne's in a friendly gesture that she knew was totally false. 'Are you bothering Mr Brewster, darling?'

'Certainly not, Mrs Hammond. I was merely asking——'

'Mr Brewster was asking if we were enjoying our stay,' cut in Suzanne hurriedly. 'I was just telling him we were having a wonderful time.'

The manager looked puzzled. 'Oh, but I——'

'Aren't we, Celeste?' Suzanne smiled sweetly at the two of them.

'But of course,' Celeste said smoothly, suspecting none of Suzanne's desperation, or if she did, putting it down to a completely different reason. She hadn't missed young Carlo slinking off as soon as she entered the hotel. 'You must be very proud of your staff.'

'Thank you, Mrs Hammond,' David Brewster said gravely before nodding to the two of them, his gaze lingering longer on Suzanne, as if he were trying to fathom her deliberate lie. Her face remained bland. 'I'm pleased you're happy here. Now if you will excuse me?'

'Certainly,' Celeste gave her most charming smile. 'What a lovely man,' she said as soon as he had moved out of earshot. 'A shame he has no money.'

'Oh, really, Celeste!' Suzanne said in disgust. 'Can't you think of anything else?'

'What else is there?'

'I can think of plenty, but none of it would interest you.'

'Probably not,' Celeste returned in a bored voice. 'Let's go out on to the terrace and have a cool drink.'

As it was what Suzanne wanted to do she raised no objection. 'Have you had a nice day?' she asked once they were both sipping their cool lime drinks, almost dreading the answer. Was it wicked to wish Celeste had changed her mind about Vidal?

Luckily it hadn't been Carlo who had brought their

drinks, but one of the other numerous foreign staff employed at the hotel. Suzanne didn't want any further trouble in that direction, not at the moment. Carlo was definitely a handsome boy, but compared to Vidal that was just what he seemed to her—young and immature.

'Don't try to divert the conversation, Suzanne,' Celeste snapped. 'I saw you with that boy. And in reception too!'

'I don't know what you're talking about.'

'Don't act the innocent with me, young lady! I told you not to see that boy again and so to spite me you meet him quite openly in reception where you can be seen by everyone. You're acting like someone out of the gutter,' she added nastily.

'And so are you, talking to me like that,' hit back Suzanne. 'You have no reason, no reason at all, to suppose that Carlo is any more to me than one of the hotel staff.'

'Well, that had better be all he is from now on. I've made contact with Vidal Martino, so you'll have to be on your best behaviour in future.'

'What do you mean, made contact? Didn't you already know the man? I thought you said you were meeting him today.'

'So I was. But by my own design.' Celeste looked very pleased with herself.

'You mean you just introduced yourself to him?' Suzanne began to realise that she had perhaps misjudged Vidal slightly. She had naturally assumed when she spoke to Vidal last night that he had known of his date with Celeste today, but now it seemed she was wrong. He was as innocent in this affair as she was herself.

Celeste looked offended. 'Nothing so crude, Suzanne. We met—accidentally.'

'And the accident was engineered by you,' she said dryly. 'So where did you go? I saw you leaving with him this morning—or at least,' she amended quickly, 'I suppose it was him.'

'Tall, dark and handsome?'

'Very,' Suzanne agreed, breathing a sigh of relief that Celeste hadn't realised she knew Vidal herself.

'Then it was Vidal. He's so charming, Suzanne, and very courteous.'

'Where did you go?'

'He took me out to lunch. To a very exclusive restaurant,' she gave a husky laugh. 'It would have to be exclusive, that's the way he lives.'

'So you really like him?' She felt her heart sink.

'Mmm, absolutely fascinating. And so good-looking!'

Suzanne did her best to smile brightly. 'So you think you'll manage to win him?'

'Vidal? Oh, I'm sure I could if I wanted to,' she chewed her bottom lip thoughtfully. 'No, he isn't going to be the problem. I could tell he liked me straight away.'

Suzanne could believe it, with Celeste looking the way she did at the moment. What man could resist her? 'So what's your problem?'

'The Conte Cesare Martino.'

'The Conte?' she squeaked. 'What—who is the Conte Cesare Martino?'

Celeste looked at her painted fingernails. 'He is *the* man, Suzanne. And he isn't as easy to get to as his brother.'

'But I—I thought—I don't understand. I thought Vidal ...'

'Oh, no,' Celeste shook her auburn head. 'Much as I would prefer that it was Vidal with the money and title I'm afraid it's his much more austere brother who has it all.'

'But what about Vidal?'

'Charming, but completely unsuitable. No, it's the Conte Cesare Martino that I intend having as my husband.'

CHAPTER FOUR

SUZANNE ate her dinner with much more relish than she had the evening before. Celeste wasn't interested in Vidal! It seemed too wonderful to be true. Since Celeste had told her this afternoon that it was the Conte she was interested in and *not* Vidal, she had felt a lightening of her heart. At least Celeste wasn't going to get him.

'Dinner was superb this evening,' she smiled happily.

'I noticed you enjoyed it,' Celeste said dryly. 'I hope you aren't prematurely celebrating getting rid of me. I told you, the Conte won't be so easy to impress as Vidal—or so easy to meet.'

Suzanne could have told her that *she* had found no difficulty in meeting him—three times to date. She just hoped she never met him again. 'But why bother with Vidal Martino at all?' she asked curiously. Celeste had been hot and tired this afternoon and not at all eager to answer questions, but that didn't stop her feeling curious. She had yet to work out where Vidal fitted into Celeste's elaborate plans.

Celeste shrugged, sipping her liqueur coffee before answering. 'I'm hoping he'll give me an introduction to his brother.'

Not so elaborate after all. 'But why not go straight to the Conte yourself?'

'Too obvious, darling. No, I thought a nice respectable introduction from the younger brother might be more in keeping with what I hope will be my future position in the Martino household. After all, it shouldn't be too difficult to impress an old man. But no, Vidal doesn't seem that enamoured of his brother, so I'll have to think of something else.'

'You think the Conte is an old man?' Suzanne looked at her stepmother strangely. Surely she had some idea what the man looked like. The Conte certainly wasn't old, only six years older than Celeste herself.

'I suppose he has to be.'

'Don't you know?'

'The Conte isn't an easy man to find things out about. All I know or care about is that he's rich and unmarried.'

'How did you find that out?'

'I was at a party about six months ago and Vidal Martino honoured us all with his presence. We didn't meet at all, but I asked a friend about him. That's when I heard about his brother. He seemed ideal.'

Just hearing about him he must have done, but the Conte certainly wasn't a man to be easily fooled, especially when he already knew of Celeste's interest in him. Celeste was in for a shock concerning the Conte, in more ways than one!

'So you decided to stay at the Conte's hotel in the hope of meeting him.' Celeste's method was now obvious to her; unfortunately it was to the Conte too, although he mistakenly thought it was she and not Celeste who was chasing him. If the determined glint in Celeste's sparkling blue eyes was anything to go by he would soon know differently.

'Not just in the hope of meeting him. I knew he would be here now, my information took me that far, I just didn't expect him to absent himself for a week. How did you know this hotel belonged to the Conte?' Celeste asked sharply, suspicion evident in her look.

Suzanne realised her mistake too late. 'I—er—I suppose someone must have mentioned it.'

'Really?' queried Celeste, deceptively sweet. 'And who might that have been? Carlo perhaps? If you've been discussing me with that——' She broke off, her attention fixed on something behind Suzanne's head

and totally out of Suzanne's vision. 'Just look at *that*!
What a fantastic-looking man! I thought Vidal was
handsome, but he pales into insignificance compared
with this good-looking devil. Take a look, Suzanne.
Isn't he magnificent?'

Suzanne was almost afraid to turn around, already
suspecting who the newcomer was. It could only be one
man. She was right, the Conte Martino! David Brewster himself was seeing him to his table, pulling out
a chair politely for the Conte's companion—a tall
brunette, her hair swept back in a sophisticated bun
at her nape, and dressed elegantly in a flowing blue
silk gown. The woman looked about the Conte's age,
and exactly what a contessa should look like. She had
the feeling that this beautiful woman had the same
idea.

She looked away quickly before the Conte saw her
interest. 'If you like that sort of man I suppose he is
attractive in an arrogant sort of way,' she couldn't
resist adding this bit. 'But I think the woman with him
thinks so too.'

'Oh, her,' Celeste dismissed her with a scornful look.
'She doesn't have an ounce of passion in her body. Pure
ice.' She continued to watch the other couple. 'Now *he*
is a different proposition. There's fire in his veins, I
can see that just by looking at him. I bet he's a fantastic lover.'

'Celeste!' Suzanne didn't like to talk about the Conte
like this. She wondered what Celeste would say when
she knew who he was. It might be quite amusing to
see her reaction. But not when she was about! 'You
shouldn't talk about people like that.'

'Don't be such a prude.' Celeste sipped her drink. 'I
bet he isn't a faithful husband.'

'He isn't married to her!' she said vehemently. She
had done it again! Why didn't she learn to hold her
tongue?

'What makes you think that?' Celeste looked at the couple with renewed interest. 'You could be right,' she murmured thoughtfully. 'If she had been made love to by him she probably wouldn't look quite such an icicle. She's probably his fiancée or something.'

'Maybe.' Suzanne didn't want to get into a discussion about the Conte. 'Are you almost ready to leave? We could go into the lounge and have a drink.'

'Not yet. I want to look at him some more. Do you think he's staying here? The manager seemed to treat him as if he was someone special. Perhaps he's a relative of the Conte,' her interest quickened.

'Perhaps,' Suzanne agreed noncommittally.

'Do take an interest, Suzanne! Do you think he could be a relative?'

'How would I know, Celeste. You're the one who is supposed to know so much about this family. I hadn't even heard of them until yesterday.' In some ways she wished she still hadn't.

Celeste wasn't really listening, her attention fixed on the man across the dining-room. 'He's looked over this way a couple of times,' she said excitedly.

Suzanne went rigid in her chair. 'He—he has?'

'Mmm,' Celeste was smiling brightly. 'I think he's interested.'

'Oh, stop it, Celeste! The poor man's probably wondering why on earth you keep staring at him.'

'With his looks he should be used to it. Such a curious combination, that dark complexion and blond hair. I suppose he must be foreign, he has that look about him, but his colouring is so unusual. He's looking again, Suzanne!' Her eyes glowed.

'Let's go, Celeste. We finished dinner ages ago. We can't sit here for ever.'

'He's excused himself and he's coming over,' squeaked Celeste. 'Can you believe it!'

Suzanne could believe it. The Conte was too polite to

actually ignore her once they had been formally introduced. She just wished he hadn't come over now,
Celeste would be furious when she found out that she
already knew both the Martino men, especially the
Conte.

The Conte stood next to their table, dressed formally
in a white dinner jacket and black trousers, he looked
just as Celeste had described him—magnificent. He
bowed politely to them both. 'Miss Hammond—*signora*,' he said coolly. 'I do not believe I have had the
pleasure of meeting your friend, Suzanne.'

Her eyes flew open wide at his casual use of her first
name. 'I—er—Celeste is my stepmother, *signore*.' Now
had come the moment of truth, and Suzanne was loath
to introduce the two. At least Celeste was too clever
to show her anger in front of the Conte. But later——!

The Conte's eyes darkened slightly. 'Excuse my mistake, Mrs Hammond, you do not look old enough to be
anyone's stepmother.'

Celeste smiled smugly. 'Thank you.'

Again the Conte looked at Suzanne, and she read
mockery there. 'Are you not going to introduce us,
Suzanne?'

She gritted her teeth. Damn the man! He was enjoying this. He must know that she wouldn't have told
Celeste of her earlier meetings with him. He was
deliberately taunting her. 'My stepmother Celeste
Hammond. Celeste, this is——' she hesitated, but was
spurred on by those mocking grey eyes. 'This is the
Conte Cesare Martino,' she said firmly.

Celeste controlled her feelings with difficulty, although her blue eyes narrowed with shock and she
looked probingly at Suzanne. 'Conte Martino?' she
questioned softly, too softly for Suzanne's liking.

'That's right,' she said more coolly than she felt. 'The
brother of Vidal.'

'Ah, yes,' the Conte nodded. 'I believe you both know my brother.'

'Do we?' Celeste asked.

The Conte nodded. 'So I believe. Vidal told me that he had met both of you here at the hotel. Are you enjoying your stay in London?' he queried politely.

Celeste seemed to have recovered her composure now and was fully in control of herself again. 'We're having a lovely time, thank you. Won't you join us for coffee?'

Regretfully he shook his head. 'Impossible, I'm afraid. I have already neglected my dinner guest long enough. I am pleased to have met you, Mrs Hammond.'

'Please, call me Celeste,' she smiled at him coyly.

'Thank you,' he said gravely. 'I hope you will also do me the honour of calling me Cesare. Now I must return to my own table. I trust I may call on you tomorrow?'

Celeste visibly preened. 'I would love that.'

'Very well,' he bowed stiffly. 'Good evening, Suzanne.'

Suzanne mumbled her farewell to him, dreading the next few minutes alone with the very angry Celeste. She wished, and not for the first time, that she had never agreed to come here. Except of course she had met Vidal. She had never met anyone like him before, but then she hadn't met anyone like the Conte before either. Two such good-looking men in one family—incredible!

'You sly little cat!' Celeste hissed through gritted teeth. 'Which one were you in the garden with yesterday evening?' she demanded fiercely. 'No wonder you didn't want to talk about it. So, which one was it?'

'Vidal, of course.'

'I don't see why you say of course—the Conte seemed to be quite friendly towards you. He called you Suzanne.'

'That was the first time,' she explained. 'I hardly

know the man, and what I do know I dislike.'

'You know Vidal better, I suppose?' Celeste sneered, her eyes sparkling with dislike.

'Perhaps,' Suzanne admitted.

'How sneaky can you get! I suppose you forced yourself on him and made an absolute idiot of yourself out there in the garden. I saw the two of you kissing. And you only met him yesterday!'

'You don't understand, Celeste. I only——'

'I know what you only! You behaved cheaply, nothing more than an easy pick-up.'

'Stop it, Celeste! I didn't do any such thing. I liked him and——'

'And I'm sure he liked you! You must have seemed so gullible, so easy to impress. And Vidal is certainly impressive. How he must have enjoyed playing with you. You silly little fool!'

'Will you leave me alone! Why do you have to be so cruel and say such horrible things to me?'

'Because you're jeopardising all my plans. You deliberately kept quiet about meeting Cesare and Vidal.'

'But you got your introduction, didn't you!'

'Maybe I did, but I certainly didn't want it through you. The Conte probably considers me to be as cheap as he does you. How can he think anything else when you act in such a fashion with his younger brother?'

Suzanne stood up, tears standing out like huge raindrops in her sea-green eyes. 'You're horrible, Celeste! I'm going.'

'You do that. Run away and hide—I'm too furious to talk to you rationally anyway.'

Suzanne rushed blindly out of the room, conscious of grey eyes following her progress. She ignored any of the anxious looks in her direction, seeking refuge once again in the delicately perfumed garden. The Conte had deliberately caused that scene, and she hated him for it. Celeste's attitude was only to be expected in the circumstances; she would probably have felt the same way herself.

'Suzanne!'

That cool voice halted her flight across the garden, but she couldn't turn, too much aware of her tear-wet cheeks to face the Conte. He must have followed her, and she couldn't imagine what his dinner guest must have thought about such an action, or Celeste either for that matter. She must have noticed the Conte following her from the room, her eyes hadn't left him since he had entered the room.

'Suzanne!' He swung her round. 'Why are you crying?' he bent his head to see her better.

She wrenched away from him, her green eyes flashing warningly. 'I haven't given you permission to call me Suzanne,' she snapped.

The Conte straightened, his expression becoming remote. 'No, you have not. Will you tell me why you are crying?'

'But I'm not,' she wiped away the tell-tale tears. 'Not now anyway.'

'But you were,' he persisted, folding his arms across his chest determinedly as he watched her. 'Was your stepmother very angry?'

'What did you expect her to be? You knew very well what you were doing when you forced me to introduce the two of you.'

'And what did I do?'

'You made Celeste very angry.'

'And that made you cry? A spoilt little rich girl like you?'

'A—a *what*?' Suzanne was astounded.

'Why the surprise? You cannot be so poor when you can afford to stay here in luxury. Like all rich women you probably consider a man with a title the ultimate goal.'

Suzanne shook her head. 'You're wrong about me, Signor Conte. I'm not rich.'

'No?' he raised a mocking eyebrow. 'Then you want money too. My, my, you are ambitious!'

'And you, Conte, are rude and overbearing. You really think that I want you, don't you? Why should I think someone as plain as I could possibly interest someone of your standing? I have no illusions about my looks. I wouldn't aspire to be a Contessa.'

He gave a half smile. 'I was not necessarily talking about marriage. You would not need to be my wife to obtain money from me, and the position of my mistress would entitle you to a certain amount of— prestige, shall we say.'

'Who with, *signore*? Other kept women who consider themselves privileged to share a rich man's bed?'

'Perhaps,' he nodded arrogantly.

'Do I take it you are offering me that position in your life?' she asked defiantly.

'And your answer if I were?'

'I haven't been asked yet.' She looked at him between lowered lashes, her sparkling green eyes shielded from him. How dared he talk to her like this! His mistress indeed! Even Celeste would baulk at such a proposition, and *she* really wanted him. Suzanne wasn't even interested in him, as she had said; she knew her limitations. Vidal was too high class for her, let alone his snooty brother.

The Conte took a step towards her, standing only inches away from her shaking body, the steady rise and fall of his powerful chest on a level with her startled eyes. 'You are a very beautiful young girl, Suzanne. What red-blooded man would not wish to visualise your naked body lying beside him, relaxed with pleasure in the aftermath of love?' His eyes had darkened almost black. 'I ask again, what would your answer be?'

Suzanne faced him with all her pent-up anger. 'My answer would be no. No, no, no! I'm not interested in being your mistress, or any other man's for that matter.'

'So you do aim for marriage.'

'No, I do not! Would it surprise you to know that you don't interest me in the slightest?'

'Would you like me to prove otherwise?' he asked, dangerously soft.

Suzanne began to back away from the determination on that hard mouth, realising that below that surface calm the Conte was very angry. 'Don't come near me,' she warned.

Two strong hands shot out and pulled her relentlessly towards him and her struggles were to no avail. For long seconds grey eyes battled with green, until at last hers faltered and looked away. But only to pass on to that firm well-shaped mouth, a mouth that seemed to be slowly coming closer and closer, until it almost touched her own. Warm breath fanned her parted lips, almost a caress in itself, and Suzanne felt mesmerised by his physical closeness.

'Tell me you do not welcome my touch, Suzanne. Tell me!'

'I—I—I can't!' she admitted brokenly.

Instantly she was set free and the Conte stood quite a distance away from her. She looked at him with bewildered eyes. 'Do not look so hurt, Suzanne,' he taunted. 'Just an experiment that paid off. I am sure my brother demanded and received much more of a response yesterday evening. But you are not immune to me, Suzanne—or to any other man who has any experience of women. You can be aroused to passion so easily!' he added with disgust.

She could be aroused to anger more easily! 'That wasn't passion *signore*, that was just sheer fright. I have never been accosted in a hotel garden by a Venetian *Conte* before. Quite an experience,' she said coldly. 'But I wouldn't recommend it on a daily basis. Why don't you go back to your mistress, Signor Conte, and try to explain to her what you've been doing out here in the garden with me for the last ten minutes.'

'I do not need to explain anything to Elena. She does not expect it and I would not offer it.'

'Then no wonder you're looking for a new mistress —complacency must be so boring.'

'Elena is not my mistress,' the Conte told her stiffly. 'She is my cousin.'

'How nice for you.'

'You are insolent!'

'Well, I like that! After some of the things you've just accused me of you have the nerve to call *me* insolent. Of all the nerve! I didn't come here to be insulted by you or anyone else. I——'

'Miss Hammond! Miss Suzanne Hammond!' The sound of the porter calling her name stopped her in mid-sentence. The man was in the lounge paging her and she entered the room quickly before he passed on to the next room. 'Miss Hammond?' He looked at her enquiringly.

Suzanne nodded. 'That's right. You have a message for me?' Oh, please let it be from Vidal and not Celeste.

'Mr Martino is on the telephone, Miss Hammond. He insisted on us paging you. Will you speak to him?'

'Certainly. I——'

'Miss Hammond will be with you in a moment, tell my brother to wait,' the Conte cut in curtly, dismissing the man with a brief nod of his head. 'So you meant what you said this morning,' he said distantly.

'About seeing Vidal?' she asked carelessly. 'Of course I meant it.'

'Then I will wish you goodnight.'

Suzanne hesitated only momentarily before hurrying

to the telephone in reception. The Conte, after giving her a last disgusted look, had turned to re-enter the dining room. She smiled at the receptionist as she indicated which telephone to use. 'Vidal?' she said breathlessly.

'Yes,' came the husky reply. 'You were surely not expecting it to be my brother?'

Hardly! 'No,' she said steadily.

'Good. I told you I would call. Did you not think I would?'

'I—I wasn't sure.'

'Because I saw your dear stepmama today? Celeste can be quite unshakable, and it was perfectly obvious that Cesare was her real interest. Were you jealous, *cara*?'

'Certainly not!' she denied indignantly. 'And I didn't mean because of Celeste. It's none of my business if you choose to take her out for the day.'

'Then why ...? Ah, do not tell me. Cesare has been busy. My dear brother has told you of my betrothal.'

'He did just happen to mention it, yes.'

'I am sure he did. But I am not yet betrothed and have no intention of becoming so. Cesare has been presumptuous. When did you see him?'

When did she see him! It would be easier to say when she *didn't*. 'He was not at work today and we happened to meet at the hotel. He thought it best that I should know.'

'He had no right! I am a grown man, I will not be treated in this way. Did he say anything else that I should know about?'

'No,' she lied.

'I will speak to him. When can I see you, Suzanne?'

'Are you sure you should, Vidal? Cesare said——'

'Cesare! Forget him, *cara*. Since when have you been on such intimate terms that you call him Cesare?' he asked suspiciously.

'Since he introduced himself to Celeste and insisted we both call him that.'

'I see. So Celeste got her wish after all. And what did Cesare think of your beautiful stepmama? Was he suitably impressed?'

'I have no idea. Your brother gives little away by facial expression.'

'I know that,' he laughed. 'So, may I call on you to-morrow?'

'If you want to. But I think I should warn you that your brother is calling on Celeste tomorrow too.'

'All the better. We can all meet together.'

'Vidal! Do you think that's wise? Your brother is antagonistic enough towards me already.'

'Suzanne, do not worry so much,' his voice lowered caressingly. 'I am looking forward to seeing you. Are you not anxious to see me also?'

'You know I am, but——'

'No buts, Suzanne. Leave Cesare to me.'

Suzanne wished she could be as confident as Vidal about his brother. She had waited nervously about the hotel all morning, evading Celeste where possible. Lunch had been an almost silent affair, with neither of them speaking unless it was absolutely necessary. Suzanne knew Celeste blamed her for not telling her about the Conte. Her surprise at his age and attractiveness could all have been alleviated if Suzanne had just mentioned him. But to do that she would have had to tell of her meeting with Vidal, and she had wanted to keep that quiet for as long as possible, a secret to cherish to herself and not be spoilt by Celeste's barbs. And by doing that she had annoyed Celeste even more. It seemed she couldn't win, whatever she did.

'Not arrived yet, then,' Celeste said sharply as she entered the lounge, sitting herself down opposite Suzanne and crossing one silky-smooth leg over the other. She smoothed down her golden brown sun-dress fitting snugly over her small breasts and narrow waist, the narrow shoulder-straps revealing the even tan she had acquired during the last week. To Suzanne she looked self-confident and very self-assured, in fact everything she herself was not.

'No.' She would not be drawn by Celeste's bitchiness.

Celeste yawned tiredly. 'Perhaps they won't come. I must say I was surprised at Vidal deciding to arrive with Cesare. They don't exactly appear to be the best of friends.'

A smile tugged at Suzanne's mouth and she couldn't contain her amusement. 'You noticed that?'

To her surprise Celeste smiled too. 'It was impossible not to. Vidal behaves like a little boy where Cesare is concerned. He was quite unbearable about him yesterday.' She looked down at her wristwatch. 'It's almost three o'clock.'

'Mmm. But the Conte did say he would see you today, and he seems to be a man of his word. They will probably both come from the office.'

'He's wonderful, isn't he, Suzanne,' her blue eyes sparkled. 'Quite an impressive figure. I felt sure he would be an old man with a middle-aged paunch. It was a very pleasant surprise when I actually saw him.'

'So you do like him?'

'Who wouldn't? Rather arrogant, but underneath that he's just a man like any other. Well, perhaps not *any* man,' she amended. 'With looks like his I can't understand why he isn't already married, or engaged at least.'

'His fiancée died.'

'Did she?' Celeste said slowly. 'I wonder if he loved her.'

Suzanne had wondered the same thing. Surely he must have done to have remained single to this age.

Vidal had said his brother was five years his senior, which made him thirty-seven, quite old in his country not to be married with a family.

'Here they come, Suzanne,' Celeste whispered. 'Aren't they two of the handsomest men you've ever seen?'

They certainly were. Both tall and dressed in light-weight suits they were the epitome of wealth and power. Vidal's cream suit complemented his dark looks perfectly and the grey of Cesare's suit matched those frosty grey eyes of his. Those grey eyes now slid insolently over her before passing on to the now standing Celeste.

'We have not kept you waiting?' he asked gravely.

Celeste gave a bright smile. 'No,' she denied huskily. 'Suzanne and I were just relaxing. Nice to see you again, Vidal,' she greeted him casually, turning once again to the Conte. 'And of course you, Cesare.'

After the first initial greeting to her stepmother Vidal had come straight to Suzanne's side, bending his long length down to her much shorter level. 'Do not look so apprehensive, *cara*,' he said deeply, 'or I will think you are not pleased to see me.'

'But I am, Vidal, you know I am.' Her eyes were huge and glowing.

'Then do I not merit a kiss?'

Suzanne's eyes flew apprehensively to his brother, only to encounter those mocking grey eyes. Damn the man, spying on her in this way! She glared at him defiantly, reaching up to put her arms about Vidal's neck before firmly placing her lips softly on his. For a moment he was stunned and then he returned the pressure.

She instantly regretted her impulsive gesture, and moved hurriedly out of his arms to meet the cold contempt of the Conte's eyes. She blushed and turned away quickly. 'What—what are we going to do today?' she asked tremulously, determined not to look at the Conte again even though his eyes compelled her to.

Vidal's hand cupped her chin and he brought her head up to meet his gaze, his brown eyes like velvet. 'I enjoyed that,' he said gently, aware of her embarrassment. 'And what would you like to do?'

'Vidal!' his brother interrupted him, stilling the caressing movement of his hand. 'Have you forgotten this is a public place!'

Brown eyes snapped with anger and Vidal's hold on her tightened. 'Mind your own business, Cesare. Suzanne was merely greeting me.'

'So I noticed,' Cesare said bluntly.

'You are too correct, Cesare,' his brother taunted.

Suzanne looked from one to the other of them, perfectly well aware that she had caused this latest argument between them. If only the Conte hadn't mocked her!

Celeste laughed, breaking the tension that was fast developing. 'Don't be cross, Cesare. Maybe Suzanne was a little over-enthusiastic in her greeting, but you must put that down to youth.'

A look of irritation crossed the Conte's face before it was quickly masked. 'You are right, Suzanne is very young. And my brother preys on babes who are too naïve to know any better.'

'Why, you——'

'Please!' Celeste looked at the two men with humour. 'You surely didn't come to see us just to argue, you could have done that quite satisfactorily on your own.'

The Conte gave a reluctant smile, and Suzanne was surprised to see how much younger it made him look. 'You are right. Is she not, Vidal?'

His brother gave a sheepish grin. 'I am sorry. Am I forgiven?' he asked Suzanne.

'Of course. I——'

'You would perhaps like to see some of London today?' the Conte interrupted her. 'You expressed a desire to see some of the town, Suzanne. You too, Celeste?'

'Well, I—— Yes, I suppose so,' Celeste agreed hesitantly. 'We haven't really had the chance to go sightseeing up to now. Suzanne had to take things easy, she hasn't been well, you know.'

The Conte looked at her sharply. 'You have been ill?'

She glared at the smug-looking Celeste. 'Not really. I've——'

'She had a bad bout of 'flu,' Celeste cut in. 'You can see how delicate she is.'

'Indeed,' he agreed. 'Then perhaps we could go alone, Celeste? I would not like to overtire your stepdaughter.'

Suzanne felt about ten years old! Celeste looked annoyed too. 'Call her Suzanne, please. Anything else sounds ridiculous.'

'And we are perfectly capable of making our own plans, Cesare. If Suzanne wishes to sightsee then *I* will take her—alone,' Vidal put in haughtily.

'That would not be correct, Vidal, and you know it. Suzanne is an unattached young girl and you would not be chaperoned,' the Conte said distantly.

'In England we don't need chaperones,' Celeste put in sharply, not at all pleased with the way things were going. She certainly didn't want Suzanne and Vidal along on her outing with Cesare.

'But we are not English, Celeste. I am thinking of Suzanne's reputation when I say it would not be correct for her to be seen alone with Vidal.'

'And what of my reputation?' She gave him a look from under lowered lashes.

The Conte shrugged. 'That is different. You have been married, whereas Suzanne is a very young girl without the protection of a male relative.'

'I see.' Celeste's lips pursed in anger. This wasn't

what she had wanted to hear at all. 'Very well, Cesare, we will all go together.'

Suzanne and Vidal were given no further choice in the matter and followed the other couple out of the hotel. It was agreed that it would be quicker to walk to the centre of town than attempt to get there by car.

Somehow Suzanne found herself walking beside Cesare, a soft murmur of conversation coming from Celeste and Vidal as they chatted together. She was very conscious of the man at her side, although she gave a good impression of being deeply engrossed with the buildings they were passing.

The Conte looked down at her. 'Will you not talk to me?'

She looked at him open-mouthed. To talk to the Conte was the last thing she wanted to do! She looked at the other two, but they were deeply in conversation about some mutual acquaintance they had just dis-covered. 'What would you like me to talk about, Signor Conte?' she asked politely.

The Conte gave a throaty chuckle and Suzanne thought what a difference his humour made to him. In fact, he was altogether more casual today, wearing a black silk shirt below the grey suit, its buttons undone far down his chest, exposing a gold medallion nestled among thick dark hairs. Another unusual fact about this man, dark eyebrows and the hair on his chest, and yet his hair was that startling blond.

'You sound so formal, Suzanne,' he rebuked her. 'Cesare is not so difficult to say.'

'It is when it sticks in your throat,' she replied tartly.

'Can we not forget our dislike for this afternoon, *cara*?' he purred, his eyes holding her gaze until she had to wrench her eyes away.

'Don't call me that!' she snapped.

'*Cara*? But why not? You did not object when Vidal used the same endearment.'

Suzanne moved uncomfortably. 'That's different.'

'I do not see why,' he replied tolerantly. 'I have been in your acquaintance almost as long as Vidal, in fact, I have probably seen more of you—literally.'

She blushed a fiery red. 'No, you haven't! I was wearing a bikini when I met Vidal too.'

'Tell me, Suzanne, where is your father?'

'My father died three years ago. Why do you ask?'

'It is not good for you to have been in the company of a woman so much older and sophisticated than you for so long without the restrictions of a male protector. You have forgotten you are a child and not up to the expectations of men, especially men of Vidal's type.'

'And your own,' she put in cattily. Really, how dare this man lecture her like this!

'And my own,' he agreed. 'And yet you are perfectly free with both of us. Has your stepmother not taught you how to behave?'

Celeste hadn't been in her life long enough at one time to teach her anything, let alone how to act with men; she relied upon her own common sense and decency to tell her that. And here was this man accusing her of being—of being——

'Do not look so indignant, Suzanne. I am perfectly well aware of how Englishwomen do not consider the conventions of life.'

'What do you mean!' she whispered crossly, keeping her voice down so that Celeste and Vidal should not hear their argument.

'I am well versed in the ways of your countrywomen,' he said bitterly. 'Of how the vows of matrimony mean nothing to you, and the ties of children even less.'

'I don't understand you,' she shook her head. 'I haven't done any of those things.'

'Not yet, perhaps. You have plenty of time to commit these atrocities.'

'Why do you hate English women so much? What have we ever done to you?'

'You, personally, have done nothing. But I have learnt of women's cruelties through hard experience. My own mother was English,' he told her harshly. 'And she did not hesitate to leave my father and myself for her young lover, a boy of twenty to her thirty. I have learnt well not to trust one of your countrywomen!'

CHAPTER FIVE

Suzanne stepped back from the harsh cruelty of his face, her green eyes darkening with apprehension. The reason for his colouring was now apparent. An English mother and a Venetian father! But what an attractive combination it had made—and a dangerous one too. This man had learnt early in his life that his mother was faithless and had apparently rejected him quite easily, and it had embittered the adult man, making his dislike of her all the easier to understand. But she couldn't be blamed for his mother's indiscretions!

'I'm sorry about your mother,' she said stiffly. 'But you can't judge every Englishwoman against her faults. It isn't fair to do that.'

'Fair!' his face darkened even more. 'Was it fair that she left behind her a broken shell of a man and a bewildered child of three?'

'She was only one woman, Senor Con——'

'Cesare!' he said shortly. 'You will use Cesare!'

'All right, *Cesare*. But just because your mother acted like that it doesn't mean we're all the same. Anyway, your father didn't waste much time marrying again— Vidal isn't that much your junior.'

'My mother was killed shortly after her flight of love, and there seemed no reason for my father not to marry again. And this time to a properly brought up Venetian girl,' he told her haughtily. 'As he should have done in the first place.'

'But then you wouldn't have been born,' she pointed out.

'Perhaps that would have been as well,' he snapped angrily. 'My father's second wife's family did not approve of the future Conte Martino being of mixed blood, and Vidal likes it even less.'

'I'm sure you can handle it,' she said dryly.

'Perhaps.' His steely eyes were narrowed against the sun's glare.

'*Cara.*' Vidal dropped back to fall into step beside her, sliding his arm possessively across her shoulders. 'Of what are the two of you talking so avidly?' he asked lightly, the hardness of his eyes belying that tone.

Suzanne wished now that she hadn't greeted him so eagerly; she was beginning to feel rather embarrassed by his possessive attitude—when it suited him, of course, like now. She moved uncomfortably, but his arm would not be shaken. 'Nothing of importance,' she answered him softly.

He grinned down at her. 'But you both looked so intent,' he persisted. 'Will you not tell me?'

'There is nothing to tell,' replied his brother. 'We were merely discussing the attractions of London.'

'I see.' Vidal frowned. 'Cesare believes this to be the most beautiful city in the world—next to Venice, of course,' he told her mockingly.

'He may be right.' Suzanne found herself siding with the Conte, out of pure perversion, she thought, although she herself found London very interesting.

Vidal grinned with good humour. 'You have found a kindred spirit, Cesare,' he mocked.

The Conte looked down at her through narrowed eyes. 'Perhaps,' he agreed.

Vidal's mouth tightened at that look. 'We will talk together, Suzanne.'

Suzanne knew it was only a ploy to get her away from his brother, but for the moment she didn't care. The Conte was too much of a personality, too forceful, too overbearing in every way, from his sensual good looks to his domineering nature.

They talked of trivialities until they reached the

city of London itself. Again Cesare seemed to be the one to guide her, the touch of his hand on her elbow faintly exhilarating and the look in his eyes causing her to quickly look away again. For a moment she had seen naked desire in those flinty grey eyes, stronger now than yesterday evening. But that was ridiculous; the Conte didn't desire her, of course he didn't.

Buckingham Palace was beautiful, much more beautiful than Suzanne had ever imagined, although the Conte appeared to be her guide once again, point- ing out things of interest to her. This arrangement seemed to suit Vidal and Celeste, surprisingly, neither of them interested in the historical beauty around them.

Suddenly Suzanne laughed, realising the irony of the situation. 'Shouldn't I be the one to tell *you* about the beauties of London?' she smiled at him. 'After all, it is my country.'

'As I am half English I can claim both Venice and England. Also, you have never visited London before have you?'

'No,' she admitted. 'I've lived in the north of Eng- land most of my life.'

'Vidal tells me you are at college there.'

'Yes.' She felt surprised that the Conte had bothered to think of her at all after their parting of yesterday.

'Studying the human body,' he said huskily. 'How strange that you should tremble so much in a man's arms when you have studied the workings of the body so intimately. Did my desire frighten you?'

'D-desire?' She looked about her quickly to see if anyone could overhear them.

Those grey eyes never left her face. 'Do not tell me you cannot tell when a man desires you?'

Suzanne blushingly looked away. Of course they had discussed such things at college, but clinically, like all the other lectures on the human body. For this man to admit to such feelings only embarrassed her—and excited her a little too, she had to admit that. 'I——' she licked her lips nervously.

'But of course you can tell,' the Conte said scathingly. 'I am not the first man to react to your slender body or the beauty of your hair. I am sure Vidal found you equally desirable.'

There was no missing the taunting edge to his voice, and she was just about to give him a cutting reply when Celeste joined them, threading her arm intimately through Cesare's. 'Couldn't you tell me a little now, Cesare?' she asked throatily. 'Poor Vidal is becoming quite jealous.'

Those grey eyes darkened momentarily. 'He has no need to be. Suzanne and I had finished our conversation anyway.'

She felt Vidal's arm about her shoulders as he drew her to his side, leading her gently but firmly away from the other couple. 'You found my brother's conversation—interesting?' he queried softly.

Interesting! That was the last thing it had been! Revealing was more the word she would have used. Vidal's resentment towards his brother was perhaps more understandable now. He considered that a true Venetian should hold the title of the Conte Martino, although anyone more arrogant and haughty than his brother she had yet to meet. She considered Cesare Martino aristocratic enough to hold any position he wanted to.

She smiled brightly at Vidal. 'Your brother knows a great deal about London and its history.'

'So he ought to, it is partly his own country.'

'So he told me.'

'I hope you will not expect me to be as knowledgeable,' he said almost sulkily. 'England does not hold the same interest for me as it does for Cesare.'

Vidal's words proved to be correct. Suzanne relying

mainly on the guide book he insisted on buying for her to obtain any information about the Palace.

She felt quite exhausted by the time they all returned to the hotel, and she knew Celeste felt the same, although the Martino men looked as fresh and alert as when they had left. Besides Buckingham Palace the Conte had shown them Nelson's column and the Tower of London, and although Suzanne had enjoyed it all immensely she knew Celeste and Vidal had been bored. Consequently she found herself more in the company of the Conte than she would have wished for, even if he was so informative.

'Why isn't your brother living with you at your apartment?' she asked, when Vidal and herself seated alone in the lounge of the hotel were having their after dinner coffee. The Conte and Celeste had decided to have their dinner at a restaurant in town.

Vidal looked amused. 'Why should he live with me? I am thirty-two years of age, I do not require a chaperone.'

She blushed. 'I didn't mean that. I——'

'I understand you, Suzanne. I am only teasing. Cesare has been in charge here during my holiday, my assistant is in hospital, so it is not a normal occurrence. He finds it easier to travel from the hotel than from my apartment. He spent all of last week visiting our hotels in the south-west of England.'

So that was why he hadn't been here when Celeste had asked about him! 'Do you travel about the country too?'

'Sometimes. But not any more now for a while, not when Cesare himself has put in an appearance. The staff will be terrified enough without my turning up too. He does this periodically to assure himself that his hotels are being run as they should be.'

'So he'll be returning to Venice soon?'

'He could be, it all depends on how much of an

effect your stepmother has on him. He has been known to change his plans to suit a beautiful woman.'

'You think Celeste has affected him that much?' She hadn't thought them that close this afternoon.

Vidal shrugged. 'They are together now, are they not?'

He had a point. Celeste and the Conte had showered and changed and gone straight out again. They had been invited too, but Vidal had said a firm no.

He sat forward, taking her hand into his own to look down at her tapered nails. 'I return to work tomorrow, *cara*. Will you miss me?'

She smiled shyly, finding the directness of both the Martino men faintly disconcerting. 'I hardly know you,' she said softly.

'Sometimes you do not need to know a person for a long time to realise you are attracted to each other, and we are attracted, are we not?' His deep brown eyes never left her face.

Suzanne sipped at her drink. 'Are we?' she said coolly.

Vidal laughed huskily. 'We are,' he told her in mock sternness. 'Tomorrow evening I will take you to the theatre. I will call for you at seven. Is that suitable?'

She had to laugh at his audacity. 'And if it isn't?' she teased. 'I could have other plans for tomorrow.'

'I would ask you to break them,' he said haughtily.

'You're arrogant, Vidal!' she gasped. 'And I'm not sure I should say yes to you, you appear to have things too much your own way as far as women are concerned.' And she meant it! Vidal was too self-confident and over-sure of her reactions to his blatant good looks. If she wasn't careful he would walk all over her—and she wasn't sure she would object!

'Now you are annoyed with me.' He looked suitably upset. 'And you will not come out with me now?'

Now she felt guilty. 'Of course I'll come, Vidal. I only——'

His face brightened immediately. 'I knew you would come, Suzanne, you were just punishing me a little for my arrogance, were you not?'

'Perhaps,' she admitted. 'You're both very arrogant, aren't you?'

'Both?' His face darkened. 'Ah, you mean Cesare too? My brother appears to occupy your thoughts a great deal. I thought you said he did not interest you?'

'He doesn't!' Suzanne felt hot and tired, and Vidal's constant jealousy regarding his stepbrother appeared to her to be totally unnecessary. The Conte could be rather overbearing at times, yes, but not enough to warrant Vidal's incessant bickering with him. It made Vidal seem like a little boy. And at the moment, for some unknown reason, she appeared to be a bone of contention between the two of them. 'You imagine things about your brother and myself that just aren't true. If you persist in these accusations I shall go to my room!'

'You would not do that!'

'Yes, I would.'

He stood up angrily. 'Then I will save you the trouble. I myself will leave. I will call for you at seven tomorrow?'

All Suzanne's anger left her. 'Yes,' she breathed huskily.

'Very well.'

'Vidal, are we having an argument?'

His body relaxed and his eyes softened as he looked at her. 'Our first,' he admitted. 'I hope it will not be the first of many. But I must leave now anyway,' he grimaced. 'I must not be late back to work on my first day back. I would see you to your room, but I am afraid it would cause a certain amount of gossip. Most of the staff employed here are loyal to my brother and have his same prudish mind. Nevertheless, I will see you to the lift doors, that would be only polite.'

'I think I'll finish off my coffee first, if you don't mind.'

'Will you not come out into the garden with me before I leave?' He looked at her imploringly.

Suzanne knew that he wanted to kiss her, and yet she felt reluctant. What if she shouldn't see the flashing lights or sounds of thunder, as she hadn't the last time they kissed? In every other way Vidal Martino was her ideal man, and yet that one thing was missing. And yet it was the most important thing!

She looked at him uncertainly. 'Not tonight,' she answered softly.

'You are still angry with me,' he stated. 'I understand.' He kissed her fingertips. 'Until tomorrow.'

Suzanne watched him leave with a faint feeling of dismay. Why had she refused? He was handsome and exciting, everything she had ever dreamed of. Maybe if she had let him kiss her again she might have felt something, maybe the flashing lights and sounds of thunder came with practice. But that couldn't be right, it should happen straight away, not be a delayed reaction.

Vidal might be everything she had ever wanted in a man, but in truth his kisses affected her no more than Robert's. Admittedly he was more polished and experienced, and his kisses evoked a certain amount of response in her, but it wasn't enough. It just wasn't enough!

She finished her coffee and wandered out into the garden. She was so confused. If Vidal was everything she had thought exciting in a man, why couldn't she fall in love with him? Because she wasn't, and that was what confused her. No one like Vidal Martino had ever entered her life before, and yet she wasn't falling in love with him!

'Suzanne?'

She stopped in her tracks. That voice! She would always know and recognise that voice. She turned slowly to face the Conte. This was the second evening she had met him in the garden, neither of them by her design. She looked behind him for Celeste, but he appeared to be alone. Her gaze returned to the Conte as he stood silhouetted in the open doorway from the lounge. He was looking his usual elegant self, dressed formally in a white dinner jacket and black trousers.

'Conte Martino?' she returned coldly.

He closed the door behind him, putting them in comparative darkness again. He chuckled softly as he moved towards her, his light hair showing startlingly blond in the moonlight, as did her own. 'You will insist on formality between us, Suzanne, but I will not be angered by it. I thought it was you out here when I saw your hair.'

She put up a self-conscious hand to her fair curls, framing her face as usual in riotous disorder. 'I see,' she said non-committally.

'Vidal has already left?' All the time he was moving closer to her, until he was so close she could smell his tangy aftershave and the cigars he occasionally smoked.

'It would appear so.'

The Conte looked down at her. 'You are on the defensive again, Suzanne,' he warned deeply. 'I am merely making conversation.'

'Where is Celeste?' she asked pointedly. 'I'm sure she would love to listen to you.'

'But not you?'

'Not me,' she agreed.

'Why do you dislike me so much? I realise I was rude to you the first time we met, but I have since apologised.'

She looked away from the seductive quality in those compelling grey eyes. 'And promptly proceeded to insult me again,' she reminded him.

'I did?'

'You know you did.' She walked away from him to trail her hand in the softly falling fountain. It adorned the middle of the garden, softly illuminated, and very beautiful. 'You accused me of chasing you for mercenary reasons.'

'And since then you have done everything in your power to persuade me otherwise.'

'So you believe me now?'

'Definitely,' he said firmly. 'A case of mistaken identity.'

She looked at him sharply. 'You—you know?'

'About Celeste?' he nodded his arrogant head. 'But of course.'

'How conceited you Martino men are!' Suzanne said shortly.

'Vidal too?'

'Yes!'

The Conte frowned. 'What has he done to you? He has not tried to force his attentions on you? Is that why you are alone here in the garden?' he demanded angrily. 'I would not have left you alone with him, but I thought you would be safe with him here at the hotel. He usually behaves himself in front of our employees.'

Her green eyes sparkled with anger. 'Since when have you been my keeper, Signor Conte?'

'Since you looked at me two nights ago with snapping green eyes, as you are doing now,' he informed her calmly.

'Since I . . .?'

'Yes,' he told her huskily. '*Has* Vidal upset you?'

'N-no,' she said uncertainly, not at all sure she liked the way the conversation was progressing. 'Where is Celeste?'

He shrugged. 'In her room, I would presume—how should I know? We parted over an hour ago.'

'Oh.'

'You sound surprised. I would not have taken her out at all but for you. I expected it to be a foursome, not an intimate dinner for two,' he said the last with disgust.

'I don't——'

'Do not think I should be talking to you in this way? Neither do I. Perhaps it would be better if I leave you now. As long as you are all right?'

'Yes, I—I'm fine.'

He bowed, once again the haughty Conte Martino. 'Then I will wish you a good night.'

'Goodnight,' she returned to his fast retreating back.

She was still puzzling over the Conte's strange behaviour the next day. Celeste had left the hotel early for the beauty salon, insisting she needed her hair and nails attended to. As Suzanne had always done her own hair and nails this seemed the height of laziness to her. She felt sure that part of Celeste's eagerness to attend one salon or another was just pure snobbery. On her return she would be full of the exalted personalities she had met while having her nails lacquered, regaling the uninterested Suzanne with all the details.

She could almost have thought from the Conte's behaviour towards her the evening before that he was interested in her himself. He certainly didn't like her friendship with his brother. But she was being ridiculous! Cesare Martino didn't like her seeing Vidal because he had other plans for his stepbrother, plans that didn't include a penniless nobody like her. But then he didn't think her penniless, even going as far as to call her 'a little rich girl' at one time, before she had told him otherwise, of course. But he must still consider her to be fairly wealthy to be able to stay at a hotel like this. She smiled to herself. If he could see her dingy room he would soon know differently. Men of his wealth probably didn't even realise people existed in the poverty she had called home for the past three years.

'What do you find so amusing?'

She looked up with a start, her eyes widening as she took in Cesare Mártino's casual appearance. Accustomed as she was to seeing him only in well-cut suits, or his impeccable evening clothes, his faded denims and half unbuttoned navy blue shirt came as something of a surprise. A pleasant one, she might add, making him more approachable and much less the 'Conte Martino'.

She blinked twice before answering him. 'Sorry?' she finally asked vaguely.

'You are walking about the place with a big smile on your face, and although I may find it pleasing, I can only wonder at the reason for it.' He fell into step beside her.

'It was you, actually,' she answered truthfully.

'I?' He looked astounded. 'What have I done to cause you this amusement?'

She shook her head, the smile reappearing at his indignation. 'You haven't *done* anything. I was just wondering what you would think of my life as a student.'

'I would not approve. Celeste has told me that you insist on living in the same disorder as your fellow students, and that you refuse all her offers of help. I think that is perhaps taking your wish to feel one of them too far.'

Dear Celeste! She certainly wasn't taking any risks. This way, if she should happen to unwittingly give out any real facts of their living arrangements, dear Celeste would already have covered herself. What a clever, devious woman she was! 'I see. Then you don't approve of my living in a room almost starving to death?'

He frowned heavily. 'No, I do not! It was foolish to make yourself ill through pride.' He looked at her too-thin body. 'You are too delicate, too frail to survive those conditions.'

Suzanne grinned outright now. 'I hate to disagree with you, Conte—er—Cesare.' She saw his nod of approval. 'But I'm as tough as old boots.'

'As *what*?'

She chuckled at his expression. 'It's a saying we have. It means I'm as tough as leather.'

'How charming!' he said dryly.

'But I am,' she insisted. She could have added that she had had to be, but thought better of it.

Without her being aware of it he had manoeuvred her out of the doors of the hotel and was now in the process of opening the car door for her, a low sports car. It was very sleek, only a two-seater, the canvas roof lowered in the heat of the day.

Suzanne looked up at him questioningly. 'Where are you taking me?'

'We are going out for the day. You look as if a little fresh air would not come amiss. Come on, get in. I am not abducting you.'

She did as he asked, settling back in the low leather seat. She had never been in a sports car before and was amazed at how low to the ground she felt. The Conte handled the car with complete assurance and she watched him with a certain amount of fascination. He seemed different today, more at ease, a slight smile on those well-formed lips.

He turned to look at her, raising his eyebrows at her intent gaze. 'Is anything the matter?'

She blushed. 'No, nothing. Why?'

He shrugged his powerful shoulders. 'You appear to be staring at me.'

'Yes,' she admitted huskily.

'Would you mind explaining why?'

'Oh, I . . .' she looked confused. 'I don't know why. Perhaps because you seem different today.'

'How different?'

'It's hard to explain. Perhaps—perhaps it's the clothes,' she said in a rush. Denims and a casual shirt certainly weren't the attire she had ever expected to see him in.

'My clothes?' he frowned. 'But they are not so very different from your own.'

Which was true. She had taken advantage of Celeste's absence today to wear the hated denims and a green vest top. 'That's right,' she agreed. 'But I didn't intend wearing mine about the hotel. Celeste wouldn't like it.'

'But we are not at the hotel.' He changed gear smoothly as they joined the motorway stream of traffic. Most of the traffic appeared to be going into town, not leaving, allowing him free acceleration, which he took advantage of. 'And Celeste is not likely to find out,' he continued. 'She is out for the day.'

Green eyes widened. 'How do you know that?'

He smiled. 'I make it my business to find out these things.' He looked at her wind-tousled hair. 'Would you like the roof up?' he asked politely.

'Oh no.' Her eyes glowed. 'I love the feeling of freedom all this sunshine and fresh air gives me. I'm enjoying the wind in my hair.'

'Good,' he nodded his satisfaction. 'Already your cheeks have more colour and your eyes are no longer shadowed.'

She blushed at his observations. He didn't miss much. 'Where are you taking me?' she asked.

'You have heard of the New Forest in your Hampshire countryside? It is very beautiful there this time of year.'

'I've heard of it,' she acknowledged. 'And that's where we're going?'

The Conte glanced at her fleetingly. 'Do you want to go?'

'I'd love it,' she enthused. 'There should be some young foals there now.'

'Yes.'

'Will you—— Do you think you'll enjoy it? I-It doesn't seem to be the sort of thing you would enjoy.'

'But I will. You will be there, will you not?'

'Yes.' She was completely puzzled by his behaviour. He had guided her into his car before she had time to collect her thoughts together, and now he was taking her out and talking to her as if they were old friends. Which they certainly weren't! 'That was the reason I was unsure of you're enjoying yourself.'

'Really? And why should I not enjoy being with you? If I had not thought we would get on together we would not both be here.'

'Are you sure you didn't just invite me because you had nothing else to do?' she asked daringly.

His head rose haughtily. 'I have plenty of other things I could be doing at this moment.'

'Then why aren't you doing one of them?'

He shrugged. 'I felt like taking a day off.'

'And you chose me to help fill your day,' she said cuttingly. 'I'm only sorry Celeste wasn't available.'

'I would not have brought her even if she had been.'

She lapsed into a sulky silence, speaking a long time later when a thought suddenly occurred to her. 'After all the fuss you made yesterday about Vidal and myself being chaperoned don't you think our outing together is rather improper?'

'Perhaps.'

'Then you do think we should be chaperoned?'

'No. I——'

'Oh, Cesare! Look!' She clutched at his arm impulsively. 'Oh, aren't they adorable!'

For the past few minutes they had been driving through rich green woodlands, and they had just driven into a peaceful clearing, a group of horses grazing quietly together in the sunshine. Huddled close to their mothers were three young foals, their coats thick and fluffy, their noses wet and shiny, and their eyes huge and gentle.

'Oh, Cesare!' Suzanne repeated, her eyes softened with pleasure. 'Aren't they beautiful?'

He slowed the car down, pulling on to the side of the road to allow her to see the mares and foals better. 'They are very attractive,' he nodded agreement. 'But not to be petted and fed like a domestic animal,' he added warningly.

'Oh, I wouldn't do that. Anyway, it's against the law to feed them.'

'That is only right. They are born wild horses and should be allowed to continue to live that way.' He too watched the young foals' antics as they scampered around their mothers, smiling slightly at their legs too long for their body.

'Oh, I agree with you.' Her eyes glowed and she smiled gently.

One dark eyebrow rose in surprise. 'You do?'

Suzanne looked at him. 'But of course I do.' she laughed at his expression. 'It may seem as if I disagree with you on everything through sheer obstinacy, Signor Conte, but I can assure you, I don't.' She grinned impishly.

'You surprise me. And a moment ago you managed to say Cesare very charmingly.'

'Oh, did—did I?' She blushed prettily.

'You did. And I would appreciate it if you could continue to do so. You are ready to drive on further?'

She nodded her agreement, exclaiming enthusiastically at each group of horses they came to, and there were many. Suzanne had heard of the wild ponies of the New Forest, but she hadn't realised there were so many of them. There were a lot of young foals too and many mares in foal, ready to give birth any day now.

To her surprise she was enjoying herself—surprise because she had never expected to enjoy any encounter she
had with the Conte. But he made a charming companion when he cared to be, and at the moment he definitely cared to be. Her cheeks glowed and she smiled
happily as Cesare drove slowly along the narrow roads
of the forest, occasionally drawing on to the side of the
verge as they met cars coming along the other way.

His strong brown arms manoeuvred the car with a
sureness that was totally habitual, and he was as relaxed in his seat as she was. He glanced sideways at her.
'Hungry?' he asked softly.

All morning she had been denying the rumbling of
her stomach. She hadn't bothered to have breakfast this
morning and now she was regretting her omission. A
pot of coffee had seemed sufficient at the time, but
now, miles from anywhere, she longed for food of some
sort. Just the thought of it made her mouth water.

'Very,' she admitted laughingly.

They drove on for another five minutes or so before
the Conte veered the car off the road and into one of
the parking areas provided in plenty by the Forestry
Commission. He slowed the car to a stop before switch-
ing off the engine and turning in his seat to look at
her puzzled face.

'Is this suitable?' he queried.

Suzanne looked about her at the deserted but beautiful woodlands, loving the way the sun shone through
the denseness of the trees. 'Suitable for what?' she
frowned.

Cesare Martino stepped out of the car, coming round
to open her door for her. 'For our picnic, of course,' he
answered her question. 'I had the hotel pack us a picnic
lunch.'

CHAPTER SIX

SHE looked up at him as he assisted her out of the low car. 'You did?' she couldn't help sounding surprised.

He pocketed the car keys, opening the boot and lifting out a wicker picnic basket and a folded groundsheet before turning to smile at her. 'Could you please carry the cooler box?'

Suzanne lifted up the light plastic box, following him as he walked across the grass and through the trees as he looked for a suitable spot for their picnic. The place he finally stopped at seemed perfect, and it didn't take Cesare long to lay down the groundsheet.

She sat down beside him as he began unpacking the food. 'What's in here?' she indicated the cooler box.

'Wine,' he answered, preoccupied with his task.

She raised her eyebrows. He certainly didn't believe in doing things by half measures. 'I see.'

Grey eyes rested on her averted face. 'The wine is simply to add to our enjoyment of the meal,' he said coldly. 'You do not have to have any if you do not want it.'

'How could you be so sure I would come? All this food may have gone to waste.'

'I doubt it. I would have simply come on my own. I enjoy the peace I can find here, the being among complete freedom of animals. In this part of the country the horses rule. I like that.'

'So do I.' She leant back against a tree, her eyes turned dreamily up to the blue sky. 'It's lovely here. I just didn't realise anywhere as beautiful as this existed so close to London.'

Cesare removed the cork from the bottle of the wine

with ease. 'You have not travelled very much?'

She laughed lightly. 'Manchester's about my limit.'

'But Celeste said she had visited America and many places in Europe. You did not accompany her and your father?'

'No,' she answered shortly, taking over from him in the serving of the food. There were cold meats, chicken, beef, pork, and mixed salad, cheese, and fresh fruit. And of course, the wine, which she soon found was deliciously cool.

'You were at school, I suppose? It is not good to upset a child's education.' He too sipped the wine.

'I wasn't always at school.'

'True. Your chicken is good?' He indicated the food on her plate.

'Lovely!'

They ate their meal slowly in companionable silence, Suzanne watching a group of horses grazing a few yards away from them. They didn't seem bothered by the presence of human beings, although Suzanne didn't know if they would react as placidly if they attempted to get closer to them.

The remnants of the meal cleared away and only the wine left to drink, the two of them relaxed back on the groundsheet. Suzanne gazed sleepily up at the deep blue sky, her glass held casually in her hand.

'I've enjoyed today,' she said suddenly, surprising herself with the truth of her words. It had been enjoyable, a day apart.

Cesare lay beside her a short distance away, leaning on his elbow as he looked down at her. 'It is not over yet.'

She turned to look at him, wholly aware of how near he was, of how easy it would be to reach out and touch his muscular arm only inches away from her own. But she didn't want to touch his arm! Why should she? Cesare Martino meant nothing to her. Just because today he seemed like any other man of her acquaintance that was no reason to believe he could ever be anything other than the Conte Martino, a haughty aristocratic man who believed her to be after his brother regardless of his impending engagement.

She moved away from him slightly. 'It must be getting quite late.' She looked at her bare wrist. 'Oh, damn! Could you tell me the time, please?'

'Almost three o'clock,' he answered her. 'You do not have a wristwatch?'

'I do. At least, I did,' she blushed prettily. 'I went for a swim this morning. Unfortunately I forgot to take off my watch—it wasn't waterproof,' she added ruefully.

'That was very careless of you. Was it an expensive watch?'

'Oh, no,' she smiled. 'I couldn't afford anyth——' she stopped herself. 'It was just a cheap one. I have a habit of breaking them.' She had almost let Celeste down then, not that she thought for one minute that the Conte would fall for Celeste's plan to entice him into marriage. Hadn't he as much as said so himself?

'I see.' He took the empty glass out of her hand, placing it beside his own in the hamper. Those curiously grey eyes moved slowly over her face, compelling her to look at him too, even though she didn't want to. He was so close now she could see the different shades of his eyes, that light grey that could darken almost to black, and the strange gold flecks surrounding the pupils.

All the time he was coming closer and closer and Suzanne felt mesmerised by the dark brooding look in his eyes, and those firm slightly parted lips that slowly lowered on to hers as he bent his head. Suzanne was unprepared for this caress and her mouth parted involuntarily at the demanding pressure of Cesare's.

Everything seemed to be happening slowly, as if in a dream. All Suzanne could register was sweet searing pleasure, a floating sensation beyond description. Celeste was right, lights didn't flash, and there were not sounds of thunder, there was just complete removal from reality.

She turned into Cesare's arms, her hand moving up his chest to caress his shoulders and the thick column of his neck. Her fingers ran through the hair that grew low over his collar, loving the feel of his strong muscular body beneath her touch. His lips moved firmly against hers, demanding and receiving a response that was completely without reserve.

Cesare moulded her body against the hardened muscles of his thighs, his hands running experimentally over her hips and slowly up over the taut nipples that pushed responsively against the thin vest top. One hand lingered to explore the intimacy of her body before slowly trailing back down to her thighs, his fingers digging into the softness of her flesh as he strained her closer.

His lips wrenched away from her clinging mouth and he buried his face in her bubbly curls. 'You enticed me into this, *cara*,' he muttered throatily, raining kisses wherever his lips alighted.

'I did?' she asked softly, her lips slowly caressing his chest where several buttons of his shirt had come undone under her questing hands.

'You did,' he agreed firmly. 'You with your green eyes that beckon and beguile, and tempt a man to find out if you taste as sweet as you look,' he groaned against the smoothness of her throat.

'And?' she questioned breathlessly, lying back now as he bent over her.

'You taste sweeter, much sweeter.' Once more his mouth descended on to her own, and she knew herself lost again. 'So much sweeter than I ever believed possible.' He parted her lips to probe the moistness of her mouth, curving her body up to meet the demand of his own. 'Tell me, *cara*, if I asked you to be with me tonight would you come to me?'

She looked away from those probing grey eyes, wanting to say yes to anything he asked of her. She knew now that this was the man she had been searching for all her life, the man who had shown her heaven with the touch of his lips. He was the reason she couldn't react to Robert or Vidal, or any other man. He was the man of her dreams, not dark-haired and velvet-eyed at all, but silver-blond with all too seeing grey eyes. He was the Conte Cesare Martino, and she loved him.

Complete panic entered her eyes and she moved hurriedly out of his arms. She wasn't a fool, she knew that when he asked her to come to him that was exactly what he meant, and nothing more. He was a man who took a mistress at will and discarded her as easily, a man who would use her and throw away what was left. And there wouldn't be much, just a shell of a girl still in love with a man who didn't want her.

But how had it happened? *Why* had it happened? Until a few minutes ago she had been happily contemplating her date with Vidal that evening, confident of his growing affection for her. And now everything had changed. She would never be the same again, never *feel* the same again. And tonight she had to spend the evening with Vidal, all the time wishing she were with his brother, no matter how tragically it might end for her.

She looked at Cesare now, wishing she could say yes to him, but fearing the outcome. She had never gone further than a few lighthearted kisses, Vidal's embrace of two nights ago the nearest she had ever come to experiencing such soul-shattering kisses. And yet in Cesare's arms she had come alive, sensually alive to the demands of her own body. And it frightened her, made her completely vulnerable to this ruthless man's moods.

Looking at him now she could hardly believe the

passion they had just shared. She felt sure her hair was more unruly than normal, that her eyes were over-bright and feverish, her cheeks aflame, and her lips still throbbed from the urgency of his kisses. And yet apart from those few extra buttons undone on his shirt and a certain rakishness to his hair, Cesare seemed completely unmoved. She felt shattered, and he looked as calm as usual! He had just upset her whole world, he had no right to look so calm and composed!

Because of her resentment she answered more sharply than she intended. 'I have to get back,' she told him stiffly. 'I'm going out at seven o'clock.'

'With Vidal?' She was no longer looking at him, so she missed the tightening of those well-shaped lips.

'Yes, with Vidal,' she told him shortly. 'Do you have any objections?' she asked defiantly.

Cesare stood up in one little gesture. 'I have plenty, but now is not the time to go into them. Come,' he packed up the hamper, 'I would not have you arrive late for your date with Vidal.'

After folding up the groundsheet she followed him miserably to the car. They drove in silence for perhaps ten minutes before he gave an impatient sigh. 'Would you like me to apologise?' When she didn't answer him he looked at her sharply. 'Suzanne?'

She cleared her throat huskily. 'No.'

'Then what do you want?' he demanded roughly.

'Nothing.'

He let out an expletive in his own language before lapsing into silence himself. One glance at his taut angry face warned her not to say another word. What would be the good of telling him she was angry with herself and not with him? She was angry and confused and in love with a complete stranger! At least, her body recognised it as love, the rest of her didn't feel too sure about it. How could she love someone she didn't really know? It seemed incredible.

By the time they reached the hotel she had convinced herself she had imagined it all. No one fell in love just at the touch of another person's lips. She was being silly and impetuous, and allowing the Conte's experience and sensuality seduce her into believing the unbelievable.

The Conte opened the car door for her, bending low over her hand as he said goodnight. 'I hope you enjoy your evening with my brother,' he said harshly.

Suzanne looked for some softening towards her in those steely grey eyes, and found none. 'Thank you,' she replied softly. 'And thank you for taking me out today.'

'Very politely said,' he mocked. 'I notice you did not repeat that you enjoyed yourself.'

'Oh, but I did!' she exclaimed. 'At least——'

'The first part of the afternoon,' he finished for her. 'I will not lie, I enjoyed all of it. I hope it can be repeated some time.'

Suzanne stiffened at his intended mockery. 'I doubt it.'

'I would not be too sure of that fact.'

She wasn't sure, she wasn't sure at all. Her anger at herself for her weakness concerning this man took her all the way into the reception of the hotel. Why should a few kisses have affected him, she was being stupid to expect them to.

'Suzanne!'

Oh, lord! She turned slowly to face Vidal. Oh, goodness, Celeste was with him. And they both looked furious! Perhaps with good reason, without her being aware of it Cesare had followed her into the hotel. And there could be no doubt that Vidal and Celeste realised they had come in together. Vidal looked flushed and angry and Celeste's eyes were icy cool; she wondered for how long.

She smiled uncertainly now. 'Vidal,' she greeted him shakily. 'You're early.'

'Yes,' he said shortly, those eyes that she had thought soft and seductive now narrowing suspiciously. 'I managed to finish my work sooner than expected. I came here with the intention of taking you out, only to find you had already left with Cesare.' He now looked at his brother with unconcealed dislike.

Cesare seemed unconcerned by his brother's outburst. 'I was not aware, and I am sure neither is Suzanne, that she has to ask your permission before leaving the hotel,' he said, deceptively mild, a slight smile curving those firm lips, but the eyes remained steely grey, giving lie to his calm attitude.

'I did not say she had to do so,' Vidal returned stiffly. 'But we do have a date for this evening.'

'This evening, yes,' Cesare agreed. 'But Suzanne's day was free. I am sure you have been suitably entertained by Celeste.'

'That is not the point,' Vidal insisted. 'Where have you been, Suzanne?'

She moved uncomfortably under those dark brooding eyes. 'I—we've been——'

'I hope you will all excuse me,' Cesare cut in. 'I am going to my suite. For myself I think it none of your business where we have been, Vidal, but if Suzanne chooses to tell you that is up to her.'

Suzanne watched in dismay as he turned on his heel and took the stairs two at a time, leaving her to face Vidal and Celeste alone. 'We've been out,' she told them defiantly.

'But where?' put in Celeste. 'You calmly go off and don't tell a soul where you've gone.'

'There was no one here to tell,' she answered reasonably.

'You could have left a message at reception,' returned her stepmother tautly. 'Or didn't that occur to you?'

'No, it didn't! It may have escaped your notice, both of you, but I am over eighteen and a perfectly free agent. I don't have to tell anyone where I've been *or* where I'm going!' She had been stung into anger by Cesare's scornful dismissal of her. 'Now, if you'll excuse me, I too wish to go to my room.'

'Your own room?' Celeste queried softly behind her.

She spun round. 'Yes, my room! What are you implying?' Her eyes narrowed.

'I too would like to know that.' Vidal's voice was chillingly cool and glancing at him Suzanne saw that he wasn't looking at Celeste but at herself.

She looked from one pair of accusing eyes to the other, all the time her anger rising. 'Just what do you mean, Vidal?'

He shrugged, his face still distant. 'You have been out with Cesare, what am I to think?'

'I should think it's pretty obvious what you *imagine*! I'm going to my room and I couldn't give a damn what the two of you think. I just want you to leave me alone.'

'But I—— We are going to the theatre this evening,' Vidal reminded her hurriedly.

'I couldn't go out with you after this,' she smiled bitterly. 'Why don't you take Celeste instead? The two of you seem to have so much in common that I'm sure you'll get on well together.'

She didn't wait for either of them to reply but stepped into the waiting lift, pressing the button for her floor. How dared they! She fumed silently to herself. She spent an innocent day out with Cesare Martino and they had the nerve to accuse her of being more than a casual acquaintance. Well, perhaps it hadn't been that innocent, but they weren't to know that. It had started out innocently enough.

She slammed the door to her hotel room, flouncing into the room to throw her handbag on the bed. She came up with a start. 'Oh!' her eyes widened. 'How did you get in here?' she demanded, outraged.

The Conte sat up from his lounging position in her armchair, smiling in the face of her anger. He held up a key. 'This fits that door.'

'How did you get it?' Suzanne demanded. She stood back away from him, challenge in every line of her body.

'I own this hotel, it is quite easy to get the key to any room I want to.' He watched her agitated movements through narrow eyes. 'And I wanted the key to your room—very much.'

'You—you did?' her eyes were wide with shock. 'And even if you did, it isn't very ethical.'

He laughed softly. 'Ethics do not enter into our relationship. You would not answer my plea for you to come to me this evening, so I have come here for my answer.'

'You—you've come here?'

'You surely did not expect me to just let you go like that?' he chuckled lightly. 'Oh, no, Suzanne, I would not do that. I wondered how long it would take for you to leave Vidal and Celeste in reception. I am glad I did not have too long to wait.'

'L—long to wait ...?' she repeated hesitantly. 'I don't know what you mean, but my answer to your question is no. I would have thought you would have realised that.'

He shrugged. 'Women have been known to change their minds.'

'Not me, not in this case anyway. And I want you to know that I'm getting highly fed up with your creating situations and then walking out on them.'

'Do I do that?' He seemed unconcerned by her refusal.

'You know you do.' She ran a hand through her hair,

tousling her curls into more disarray than usual. 'You did it the other evening and again just now. And it's always me you leave to sort it out.'

'And did you—sort it out, I mean?'

'Hardly,' she said dryly. 'I left them to it.'

'Completely unscathed?'

'No.' She found her gaze drawn again and again to him. He must have come straight to her room because he was still dressed exactly the same—and still looking as attractive. 'They made their displeasure felt.'

Cesare laughed. 'I am sure they did.' He stood up. 'Well, now that I know you are capable of defending yourself, and you have given me my answer, I will leave you to change for your evening with Vidal.'

'Was that what all that was about, a lesson in defence?'

'Perhaps.'

'I see. Well, you can keep your lessons to yourself. And I'm no longer going out with Vidal, this evening or any other time.'

'Because of our day together?'

'No,' she told him sharply. 'Because I couldn't stand his intolerable behaviour. Your brother doesn't own me. Now if you don't mind leaving my bedroom, I intend having a shower, and I would appreciate it if you would remove yourself. And give the key back to the receptionist, you won't be needing it again. My God, you have a nerve! Did you actually ask for my key?' She looked incredulous.

'Among others.' He brought out several more keys from his pocket.

'Oh, I see. I'm only one among many.' Her eyes glittered her anger. 'I suppose Celeste's is there too?'

That firm mouth tightened into anger too. 'And why should you suppose that?'

'Why not?' she asked flippantly. 'You said it was only one of many, so why not Celeste's?'

'These other keys are what you might call a smoke screen, to divert suspicion from the one I really wanted. And I do not happen to desire your stepmother,' he said through gritted teeth, moving towards her with determination. 'But I do desire you. You know that already, do you not?'

'I—I—— No, of course not!'

'But you do,' he said quietly. 'You have always known it. That is why I frighten you. And I do frighten you, do I not? This afternoon you——'

'Please! Don't let's talk about this afternoon. I—It—I——'

'It embarrasses you,' Cesare interrupted her stuttering. 'This afternoon,' he continued, 'you deliberately stopped our lovemaking because you were frightened. I understood that and did not pursue the subject, otherwise you might not have got away so easily.'

'So you *are* on the look-out for a new mistress,' Suzanne burst out. 'Well, don't include me in any of your plans. I'm not about to become anyone's mistress, even if you do have the key to my room.'

He held up the key. 'This? I borrowed it for the one occasion only, the next time I enter this room it will be at your bidding.'

Suzanne gasped. 'You can't imagine I would ever do such a thing? I—I wouldn't!'

Cesare moved stealthily towards her, his hands moving out to take a firm hold of her arms and pull her slowly towards him. 'Are you sure of that?' he breathed huskily. 'Your actions earlier did not point to that.' Those grey eyes never left her face and she stared at him as if mesmerised.

Her eyes moved to those firm lips, parted lips, that evoked in her a response she couldn't control. It wasn't fair of him to keep playing on her senses like this, but then why should he want to play fair when he made no secret of his desire for her?

'I want you so much, *cara*,' he breathed against her mouth, before claiming her lips in a slow languorous kiss. It was like a ravagement of her whole body, and Suzanne responded without restraint. Her body was crushed against the hardened arousal of him and she knew he meant what he said.

She also knew she hadn't been wrong earlier, all her logical thinking in the car had been for nothing. She *loved* this man. With him she reached the dizzy heights she had always believed possible, wanting only to please him in every way she could. She kissed him back unrestrainedly, running her hands caressingly over his firm muscled back.

Cesare broke the kiss to bury his face in her scented hair. '*Cara*, you are——'

'Well, Suzanne, you've done it now,' drawled Celeste from behind them. 'So you really meant it when you said you were going to your own room. What you omitted to say was that Cesare was joining you here. I didn't realise to what lengths you would go, Suzanne.' She came further into the room, completely unconcerned with the fact that she had just interrupted something between them that was totally private. 'Your quest for money has really made you desperate, inviting a man into your room in this disgusting way.' Her lips turned back in a sneer. 'And a Conte at that!'

Cesare stepped back, the desire that had been in his eyes only seconds earlier now completely shielded by his lowered lids. 'Suzanne did not invite me to her room, Celeste,' he said coldly, completely in control of himself and the situation.

'I can't believe you came here uninvited.' Celeste looked at him sharply. 'I know Suzanne of old, don't forget.'

So far Suzanne had been dazed, but this was the second time Celeste had implied that she had deliberately set out to entice Cesare to her bedroom. How utterly wrong could she be! 'What are you saying, Celeste?' Her eyes were huge with her bewilderment. What on earth was Celeste trying to do to her now?

Celeste gave a light laugh. 'Don't try acting innocent! I wish I had never agreed to bring you here now. I should have realised, should have known better. This isn't the first time I've had to break up a situation like this, Cesare. Suzanne has a habit of taking men to her bedroom. For what, I'm sure you can work out for yourself.'

Suzanne stared at her dazedly. What was Celeste *doing*? What was she saying? She shook her head. 'You're wrong about this situation, Celeste, totally wrong. I don't know why you're saying these things, why you're telling such lies.' She looked to Cesare for help, but he had withdrawn back into being the Conte Martino. How could he change so rapidly! She was still trembling from the passion they had shared. 'Cesare!' she begged chokingly.

'It's no good pretending any longer, Suzanne. I have to tell Cesare your real reason for being here.' Celeste turned to look at him. 'Suzanne has been ill, yes, but the reason she was ill was because of an unhappy affair with a married man. The man finally drew the line at leaving his wife for her and Suzanne just couldn't take it. I finally had to bring her away to stop her making an absolute fool of herself about him.'

'That's a lie!' Suzanne burst out. 'It's all lies. You can't believe her, Cesare? I've never had an affair with a married man, I've never had an affair with *any* man!'

Cesare's mouth had tightened into stern lines. 'You do not have to proclaim your innocence to that extreme. I am well aware that today's trends do not allow for morals.'

'I'm glad you see my point of view,' cut in Celeste silkily. 'Suzanne has this ridiculous idea of getting herself a rich man, preferably a single one.'

Those grey eyes narrowed even more as he looked at the elder woman. 'I did not say I did see your point of view,' his voice was icy. 'She might just have succeeded if you had not come bursting in here just now without knocking.'

Celeste gasped. 'You can't mean that? Suzanne is only a child!' Her blue eyes were becoming stormy.

His mouth quirked with mocking humour. 'But what a child!'

Celeste turned away as she began to realise things weren't going as she had planned them to. She had received the shock of her life a few minutes earlier when she had walked in here and found Suzanne held very securely in Cesare Martino's arms. She had come up here to gloat over Vidal asking her to accompany him to the theatre instead of Suzanne, and this was what she had found. Suzanne was spoiling things for her for good, and while she knew her bitchiness might thwart her own plans in this direction, she had no intention of letting Suzanne get away with her duplicity.

'And you're wrong about my knocking, Cesare.' She regained her composure. 'It appears you were both too —busy to hear me.'

Cesare nodded haughtily. 'You could be right.'

'We weren't busy at all,' interrupted Suzanne.

Celeste raised a mocking eyebrow. 'Weren't you? Well, let's say you were giving a very good impression of it.'

'You're being ridiculous,' she said, outraged. 'Both of you are. You're arguing about me as if I'm an inanimate object. I don't know why you're lying, Celeste— well, perhaps I do.' But she couldn't reveal in front of Cesare that as far as her stepmother was concerned he was her exclusive property. 'But I won't stand for it. I wish I'd never let you back into my life, wish I'd stayed in Manchester where I understood the people and the rules they live by.'

'Like having an affair with a married man,' Celeste said bitchily, her blue eyes almost spitting her dislike.

Suzanne looked appealingly at Cesare. 'She's lying!' she cried. 'Believe me, Cesare, she's lying.'

He smiled at her, but it didn't quite reach the depths of those grey eyes. 'You are making too much of this thing, both of you. I did not ask for virginity when I kissed Suzanne,' he told them coldly. 'It was a kiss, no more. And if I choose to kiss her again I do not think it is anything to do with you, Celeste.' His voice had hardened into anger.

'Oh, but——'

'Leave it. I just want you to realise that one dinner together does not entitle you to question my movements.'

'But I——'

'You will not interfere again!' he snapped, before turning to look at the pale Suzanne. He held up the key to her room. 'Remember what I said about this.' He dropped the key softly on to the side table and after giving one last cold look in Celeste's direction, let himself out of the room.

'Well!' she exploded, her face flushed with anger. 'The nerve of the man! And I actually had him picked out to be my husband. Bossy overbearing individual!'

'You did give him reason——'

'Reason be damned! He shouldn't have been in your room to start with. It isn't decent at six o'clock in the evening.'

Suzanne smiled wanly at her outrage. 'I suppose if it had been eleven o'clock *then* it would have been decent?'

'Don't be facetious! How could you give him the key to your room?' Celeste demanded. 'If you have to have a wild fling with a man at least hold out for a respectable period.'

'I didn't give him the key.' Suzanne shook her head wearily.

'Then where did he get it? No, don't answer that,' she put up a hand. 'I don't want to hear any more. You've ruined any chance I may have had with him.'

'And you've just done the same for me with your lies.' She should feel like shouting and screaming at this scheming woman, but somehow she just didn't have the energy.

'I realise that. But he would eat someone like you for breakfast, you just aren't experienced enough to cope with someone like him. Although you have more experience than I would have given you credit for. Just what have you been doing the last three years to have the knowledge to handle someone like Cesare Martino? He's no immature youth. And he wants you, doesn't he, Suzanne?'

She blushed at her candidness. 'Just how long were you in my room before you made your presence known?'

Celeste smiled knowingly. 'Long enough. And soon enough to stop you making a fool of yourself.' She smoothed her skirt. 'Well, if you will excuse me now, I have to go and get myself ready. Vidal took your advice and invited me to the theatre in your stead. It seems you've lost his affection.'

'And Cesare's,' she choked. 'When you do something, you really do it well, don't you?'

'You finished things yourself with Vidal,' she touched her hair. 'And I just didn't see why you should have it easy with Cesare. I didn't realise when I brought you here that you would ruin all my carefully laid plans. Six months it took me to get the money together for this holiday and to work out exactly when Cesare would be here. And it all went out the window the first time I saw the two of you together. He wanted you then, he's always wanted you. But I still have Vidal,' she smiled to herself. 'He's more my type, I suppose, and just as rich.'

'Vidal?' Suzanne was astounded.

'Mm,' Celeste nodded. 'We're about the same age, we appreciate the same things, and most of all—he likes me.'

Suzanne laughed chokingly. 'You're incorrigible, Celeste! You really don't give a damn, do you?'

'Oh, but I do.' Celeste patted Suzanne's shoulder. 'You'll see. If Cesare likes you enough he'll be back.'

Suzanne slumped down on the bed after Celeste had left. She was right, Cesare would be back, but what did he expect of her when he came back? The key on the table seemed larger than life and she moved hurriedly away from it. Cesare had made his position perfectly clear. He wanted her, as Celeste so rightly said, but that was all he did want. She, as a person, didn't interest him in the slightest. So much had happened to her today, Cesare kissing her, her argument with Vidal, and now this scene with Celeste, so much that she didn't know what she wanted. But one thing she knew for sure, she wasn't going to become Cesare's plaything, even if she did love him.

She lay back on her bed, her hands behind her head as pillows. Cesare's kisses made time stand still, made her feel as if the whole world shook beneath her feet, and the sky was aflame. Deep penetrating kisses that she knew would always evoke a response within her.

But he believed her to be something she wasn't, had all too readily accepted Celeste's story of her affair with a married man. Even worse, it hadn't bothered him in the slightest. He had no respect for her, and where there was no respect there could never be love. But Cesare had never mentioned love to her, only she felt that weakening emotion, and she did feel very weak and vulnerable where he was concerned.

CHAPTER SEVEN

THE receptionist stopped her on her way from having breakfast. 'Miss Hammond?' the young girl smiled.

Suzanne went to the desk. 'Yes?'

'I have a parcel here for you.' She bent under the desk to bring out a small oblong parcel. 'There's a card with it.'

'Thank you,' Suzanne smiled vaguely, wandering over to a chair in the corner. She turned the parcel over, ripping off the paper and snapping open the clasp. Inside was a small gold wristwatch on the most delicate strap she had ever seen. It was beautiful, absolutely beautiful, and she hardly dared open the card, fearing what she would read.

Her hands shook as she pulled the tiny card out of its envelope, turning it over to read the large scrawl. 'I'll be counting the minutes until we meet again. I hope you will too,' she read slowly.

There was no signature, but it wasn't necessary. Cesare had sent her this expensive gift. But she couldn't accept it, in no way could she accept it. She walked back to the desk. 'Please,' she gained the receptionist's attention, 'could you tell me where the Conte Martino is, please?'

The girl shook her head. 'The Conte isn't here, I'm afraid, Miss Hammond,' she said regretfully.

Damn! He must have gone into work today. 'Could you tell me what time he'll be back?'

'I think you must have misunderstood me. When I said the Conte wasn't here, I meant he's checked out.'

'Ch-checked out?'

Suzanne had paled drastically and her distress must

have shown, because the other girl looked quite concerned. 'I'm sorry, Miss Hammond. I didn't realise——
He could be back in a couple of days,' she added.

'He—he could?'

'Perhaps.' The receptionist answered shortly as if
realising she had perhaps revealed too much already
about her absent employer.

'I see,' Suzanne attempted a shaky smile. 'Thank
you.'

She walked dazedly out into the garden, Cesare's
message now taking on new meaning. But where had
he gone? Was he away on business or pleasure? No
matter which it was she had no right to question him
about it.

She had intended returning back home today, but
she couldn't go now, not without saying goodbye to
Cesare. But how could she stay? Celeste didn't need
her here now, and she had no money with which to pay
her own bill. The thought of having to return to her
sparse tiny room was totally repugnant to her.

Celeste came floating out to the poolside, and floating just about described her. She was glowing, her
beauty unmarred by cosmetics as it usually was, the rosy
hue on her cheeks due to nature and not make-up.

'Good morning, Suzanne,' she greeted cheerfully.

'Good morning,' she returned dully. 'I've already
breakfasted.' If a pot of strong coffee could be called
breakfast. She had had no appetite for food this morning.

'I'm not hungry,' Celeste smiled happily. 'Isn't it a
wonderful morning?'

'If you say so.'

'Oh, I do. Cheer up, Suzanne. Are you still annoyed
about yesterday?'

'I don't have any right to be, do I? When would you
like me to leave?' she asked resignedly.

'Leave?' Celeste's blue eyes sharpened with interest.

'Why should I want you to leave? I thought you liked it here.'

'I do. But I—— You can't want me to stay now. I didn't deliberately ruin things for you with Cesare— it just happened.'

'Oh, Cesare.' Celeste dismissed him with a wave of her hand. 'I know the first time I met him in the dining-room that he wouldn't be duped by my little act. He's far too shrewd. Although he doesn't yet realise we're both broke. If I'd known what he was going to be like I wouldn't have bothered with him at all. I thought he would be an older man, grateful for the attentions of a younger woman. He's only six years older than me,' she added in disgust.

'But you thought he was handsome.'

'I still do. All that arrogance and cynicism, he's fascinating. But I would probably bore him within a few days. I'm not clever enough for him.'

If Celeste would bore him what would she do! She was so much younger than him, and immature for her years too. No, he found her body desirable, but her mind wouldn't interest him at all. 'Neither am I,' she admitted miserably.

'Goodness, you are down today, aren't you.' Celeste picked up the jewellery box from her lap. 'A prezzie?' she arched an eyebrow.

Suzanne nodded. 'One I intend returning.'

'Oh, I see.' Celeste opened the box. 'Wow!' Her eyes glowed as she picked up the watch to look at it more closely. 'It's beautiful!'

'Mmm,' Suzanne reluctantly agreed with her.

Celeste put it on her own wrist, admiring the small-ness of the face and the ease with which the strap fitted, so light it was hardly noticeable. 'From Cesare?'

'Yes.'

She gave a throaty laugh. 'I told you he would come around, and much quicker than I imagined.'

'I don't think so,' Suzanne shook her head. 'I think it's in the nature of a parting gift.'

'There was a card with it?'

She handed it over reluctantly. The message didn't read like a severing of their friendship. But surely Cesare didn't really expect to have an affair with her? He couldn't want anything else after the impression Celeste had given him of her morals. But she couldn't wholly blame Celeste; Cesare had already made his feelings towards Englishwomen known to her, and they weren't good. His own mother had let him down badly, and he wasn't likely to forget that. So any daydreams she might have had in his direction would have to remain just that—dreams.

Celeste handed her back the card and the watch. 'It doesn't sound like goodbye. He sounds anxious to see you again.'

'Perhaps he is. But I'm not like that, Celeste, no matter what you might think.'

'It isn't what I think that counts, it's what Cesare thinks. I'll have a word with him if you like, explain to him I was only being my normal bitchy self,' Celeste smiled ruefully. 'It's something I'm good at.'

Suzanne smiled too. 'It doesn't matter, Celeste. You can't tell Cesare anything, he isn't here. The receptionist said he's left for a few days.'

'To go where?'

She shrugged. 'I have no idea.'

Celeste stood up. 'I'll call Vidal now and ask him. He's bound to know where his own brother has gone.'

Suzanne grabbed her arm to stop her exit. 'It doesn't matter. I'd rather not know. Tell me about Vidal,' she changed the subject on to something less painful for her.

The glow came back into Celeste's face. 'He's quite wonderful, Suzanne.' Her eyes became dreamy. 'And he doesn't seem to care that I'm not very clever and can be a bitch when thwarted. I had a wonderful time last night. We went out to dinner after the theatre.'

'And you really do like him?' Suzanne wasn't really surprised at the affinity between these two; they were very much alike in many ways, both seemed to like good times and neither liked too strong an emotional tie put on them. And without being bitchy, she had to admit that they were both shallow people.

'I really do like him,' Celeste confirmed. 'I'm meeting him again this evening. Suzanne, do you—do you mind about us? Usually I wouldn't give a damn about encroaching on someone else's property, but this time it's different. This time I—I don't know,' she looked embarrassed. 'I think it could be different with Vidal. I have a feeling ...'

The next two weeks dragged by. Suzanne wasn't sleeping properly and food didn't interest her in the slightest. Celeste had asked Vidal about Cesare's whereabouts, but he didn't seem to know—or he wasn't telling. Suzanne had had plenty of time to brood the last few days, plenty of time because she had been alone most of the time.

Vidal had taken advantage of his brother's absence to take a few days off work, escorting Celeste on her shopping expeditions and spending each evening with her. They had even invited Suzanne to join them for dinner one evening, going to one of the well-known restaurants that seemed to exist in abundance in London. She had refused at first, but they had insisted so much that in the end she had given in. They had gone on to a nightclub later and she had to admit that she had enjoyed their company. Celeste visually came alive in Vidal's company, and she almost forgot to be cynical.

But the last few days had begun to tell on Suzanne; the strain of pretending Cesare's absence didn't bother her was beginning to show in the dark smudges beneath her eyes and the slight loss of weight. It was weight she couldn't afford to lose, being much too thin to start with.

She spent a lot of her days wandering about the town, window-shopping and feeding the birds in the square. She should have felt lonely, but she didn't, most of her time spent thinking of Cesare and wondering what he was doing.

On the Monday of the third week of his absence she came in quite late for dinner, bumping into someone in her hurry to get to her room and change. 'Oh, sorry!' she gasped apologetically. 'I didn't see—Robert!'

'The one and only,' he grinned at her, holding her at arm's length. 'Hey, what have you been doing to yourself?' he frowned.

She hugged him, laughing happily. 'That's nice! You haven't seen me for three weeks and already you're insulting me!' She put her hand through his arm. 'How did you get here? Are you staying long? *Where* are you staying?'

'I came down on the train, I'm staying a couple of days, and I'm booked into a cheap boarding house round the corner. Your stepmother seemed to think you were lonely, so I——'

'Celeste? Celeste's been in touch with you?'

'Well, we did meet that time, and although she doesn't approve of me she seemed to think you needed a friend right now. Otherwise she wouldn't give me the time of day,' he grinned uncaringly, the freckles that often go with red hair giving him a boyish look.

She looked at him anxiously. 'But what about Patsy? You know how upset she gets if you go away. Look at the time we went to Wales for the week—she looked terrible when we got home.'

'She should be okay for a couple of days. I left her in the care of Mrs Holmes, you know how they get on together.'

Robert owned a Siamese cat called Patsy. He had found her as a four-week-old kitten, roaming about the streets crying for her mother. Advertising hadn't brought forth her owner, and this was possibly because she had a slight defect in one of her hind legs, causing a very slight limp. Consequently Robert had kept her, and she had become very possessive of him in the process.

The previous year, when Patsy was just over a year old, eight of them from the college had gone to Wales for a two-week hiking holiday. After only a week Robert had had to return home, Patsy was pining for him so badly. Suzanne had returned with him, because strictly speaking she was supposed to be his partner, and also she was very fond of Patsy herself.

'You're sure she'll be all right?' She frowned.

Robert grinned. 'Of course she will. It will probably do her good to realise I can't be at her beck and call all the time. I haven't forgiven her for ruining our last holiday together yet. She'll probably appreciate me more for this separation.'

'You are cruel, you know how much she loves you.'

'Mm, but she's very restricting at times, as we very well know.'

'Yes.' Last summer wasn't the only time Patsy had ruined their plans. With an intelligence that most Siamese cats seemed to possess, she had learnt that when she wanted her beloved master to stay at home with her she only had to 'play sick', and she had learnt to use this to great advantage. And poor Robert usually fell for it, never knowing whether the illness was real or simply put on, staying at home with his 'sick' cat, much to her delight.

'Don't worry about her, Suzanne. I'll soon know if she isn't all right,' he grimaced. 'And no doubt she'll find a suitable way to make her displeasure felt.'

'No doubt,' she laughingly agreed with him. 'So when did you arrive?'

'At the hotel? Oh, about five minutes ago. I was just asking for you at the desk when this gentleman——'

Suzanne's eyes flew to the man standing to one side of the reception area. Cesare! Her eyes began to glow, until she saw the contempt with which he was looking at the two of them, and the light suddenly died out of her face leaving her paler than ever. There was no gladness to see her there in that cold harsh face, and she wished now that she had already returned to Manchester.

'Suzanne,' he nodded stiffly. 'I am afraid I did not have the chance earlier to introduce myself to your— friend. Cesare Martino,' he nodded coldly.

'Robert Thompson.' Robert put his hand out politely to be shaken firmly by the other man.

'*Conte* Cesare Martino,' Suzanne put in pointedly.

Robert's eyes widened. 'Conte?' he repeated dazedly.

'Cesare will do,' the other man said haughtily. 'Your —friend . . .' again that slight pause and Suzanne looked at him sharply, 'Mr Thompson was asking for you. As I had already done so myself I thought it only fair to tell him you had gone out. Celeste said you had gone to the Park.'

'That's right.' A slight catch in her voice made her sound shaky. 'You were asking for me?' she asked Cesare.

He shrugged his wide powerful shoulders. 'It was not important. I will speak to you at a more—convenient time.' With a polite but frosty smile at the two of them he excused himself.

'Oh, but——' Suzanne looked at his retreating back, her distress evident in her candid green eyes. She turned to Robert, clutching his arm as if for understanding. 'I won't be a minute, Robert. You won't go away?'

At least his grin was normal, and she felt she needed

normality at the moment. 'I'll be fine,' he assured her.

She caught up with Cesare at the stairs, part of her brain hysterically registering that he never seemed to use the lifts. 'Cesare,' her voice came out husky and uncertain, and she cursed herself for her stupidity.

He turned to look at her, raising one dark haughty eyebrow. 'Yes?' His tone wasn't encouraging.

'You said you'd been asking for me,' she said breathlessly.

'So?'

'So I'm here.' Her eyes were pleading.

If anything he became more withdrawn. 'I also said it could wait until a more convenient time. Your— friend must be becoming impatient.'

'Why do you keep saying *friend* like that?' Anger at his dismissive tone entered her voice. 'That's the third time!'

'I was not counting. As to why I call him that, that is what he is, is he not?'

'Yes, but——'

'Then you have answered your own question.'

'It's the *way* you say it,' she insisted.

'I am sorry if you do not like it. I will endeavour not to do it again,' he turned away.

'Cesare, *please*!'

'Please *what*?' His eyes glittered a dangerous metallic grey. 'Do you not think it advisable to deal with one lover before you attempt to interest another? After all, he has left his wife at home to visit you here. Because you are *lonely*!' he added in disgust.

She couldn't gather her thoughts together; she didn't understand what he meant. 'Wife? What wife?'

Cesare's mouth turned back in a sneer. 'Do not pretend with me, Suzanne. I did not intentionally listen to your conversation, but it was impossible not to overhear some of it. Are you not ashamed of yourself? But of course you are not! My first assumption of you was correct—you are completely permissive, utterly without morals!'

She shook her head. 'Y-you're wrong. I don't understand what you're talking about.'

'I thought my meaning was perfectly clear,' he said chillingly. 'I abhor your behaviour with this man, can find no excuse for it. Now if you will excuse me.'

'Oh, but——'

He didn't look at her again but walked unhurriedly away. Suzanne walked shakily back to Robert's side, her eyes huge and very bewildered. What on earth was Cesare talking about? Robert didn't have a wife! Surely he didn't think Robert was this married man Celeste had referred to? Surely not; he had no basis for such an assumption, none at all.

Robert touched her arm, bringing her back to an awareness of her surroundings. 'All right?' he asked gently.

'What? Oh—Oh, yes.' She gave a bright smile that wasn't fooling anyone, especially Robert, who had known her for the last three years.

'Quite an impressive man,' he remarked casually.

'Mm? Oh—the Conte? Yes—Yes, he is.'

'I didn't realise you had exalted friends.'

This time her smile was genuine. 'I don't. He's Celeste's choice of a husband—at least, he was. I think she's changed her mind.'

'So who's the lucky man now?'

'Don't be cynical, Robert. Let's go into the lounge. Would you like tea or something?' she asked, remembering her manners.

'Tea would be fine.'

The tea was ordered, they both went into the lounge, picking a table that overlooked the pool. Suzanne was still shaking from her encounter with Cesare. Two weeks now he had been away, and when he came back they had had another argument, one she didn't even understand.

'Nice hotel,' Robert remarked.

'Yes,' she agreed huskily. 'Conte Martino owns it.'

'He must be a rich man. But of course he is if your dear stepmama thought him worthy enough to marry her. You haven't told me who she has on her hook yet,' he reminded her.

'As charming as ever, I see,' Celeste remarked from behind him, waving him back down as he made to rise politely. 'I'm glad you could come, Robert. Suzanne's looking better already. Although the same can't be said for Cesare. I've just seen him and he looks like a thundercloud. He was barely civil.'

'Suzanne just introduced me to him.'

'Did she now?' One eyebrow rose. 'So that's the reason for his bad mood.' She looked at Suzanne. 'I hope you didn't mind my sending for Robert, but you've looked so miserable the last few days, and for some inexplicable reason you find his company amusing.'

'Thanks!' Robert grinned at her, completely undaunted.

'It was a lovely idea, Celeste.' And totally unlike the Celeste of old. But this wasn't the Celeste of a week ago, this was a new Celeste, a softer, more relaxed Celeste, who found time to be pleasant to Suzanne in a perfectly spontaneous manner.

She frowned. 'I thought so at the time. Now I'm not so sure. I didn't know Cesare would be returning today. I could just have made things worse.'

Suzanne didn't know how they possibly could be, but she didn't argue with her. 'Well, I'm pleased to see Robert, really pleased,' she smiled at him.

'Thank God for that! So far I haven't understood half the conversation. I thought the Conte was *your* friend?' he said to Celeste.

'I thought so too. But it seems Cesare had other ideas. Once he'd set eyes on our little Suzanne I couldn't get a look in. So I've decided to forgo the title and simply settle for money. I don't have the time or money enough of my own to do any other,' she shrugged.

'Would someone please explain what's going on?' Robert cried. 'Are you trying to tell me the Conte wants to marry Suzanne?'

Celeste laughed softly. 'I'm not trying to tell you any such thing. Marriage was never mentioned.'

'Well, he's not having her any other way!' Robert said indignantly. 'If he's dared to suggest anything less than honourable to her I'll flatten him!'

This caused Celeste even more humour. 'Oh, he's dared all right. And I hardly think your threat would exactly frighten him.'

'Please!' Suzanne put up a hand to her aching temple. 'Whether or not the Conte would be frightened isn't important, because Robert isn't going to threaten him. The Conte has made his feelings concerning myself very clear—they're non-existent.'

'That isn't true, Suzanne. I saw the two of you together that day, and I——'

'Celeste, please! I don't want to talk about it any more.'

'All right,' Celeste sighed. 'Actually I was looking for you to invite you out to dinner with Vidal and myself this evening. I suppose you may as well come too now that you're here, Robert.'

'Thanks again!' he said dryly.

'It's in the nature of a celebration,' Celeste said almost shyly.

'Oh, yes?'

'Celeste?' Suzanne looked at her excitedly. 'You don't mean—— You aren't——'

'I am—I mean *we* are,' her blue eyes shone. 'I'm so excited I can hardly think straight. Vidal asked me to marry him last night. Oh, I know we haven't known each other very long, that he preferred you first, that it's too soon to know if we really love each other. But I don't care! I've always scoffed at this shattering thing called falling in love, you know that, Suzanne. But with Vidal ... Oh, I just want to be with him. And he feels the same way.'

'I'm so pleased for you,' Suzanne said sincerely.

'You've lost me again,' Robert said dazedly. 'Who is Vidal—besides being your future husband?'

Celeste looked at him scathingly. 'He's Vidal Martino.'

'Any relation to the Conte?'

'His brother,' she answered shortly.

'What is he, Italian or something like that?'

'Something like that,' she said dryly. 'Venetian, actually. And they are so romantic, aren't they, Suzanne?'

Suzanne frowned, shrugging. 'How would I know?'

'You should do, you've kissed both of them.'

'B-both of them?'

'Mm,' Celeste smiled. 'I'm not jealous of your evening in the garden with Vidal. If it happens again I might be, but not at the moment.'

'I was hoping you'd forgotten it,' Suzanne smiled ruefully. 'I should have known better.'

Celeste pouted. 'Now you aren't going to argue with me today of all days?'

'No, of course not,' she laughed. 'How does the Conte feel about your marriage? I suppose you've told him?'

'Vidal was going to call him today, but now it isn't necessary. Vidal has invited him out to dinner with us this evening in the hope of getting him used to the idea of seeing us together.' She became thoughtful. 'I suppose he'll be all right about it. He was quite pleasant to me earlier. Not quite so polite just now, but that was your fault,' she looked pointedly at Robert.

'*My* fault? What did I do? I've only just arrived.'

'Exactly. When I spoke to Cesare earlier I don't think a boy-friend entered into his immediate plans for Suzanne.'

Suzanne remembered the seductive look in his eyes as he had put the key to her room on the table, and found herself agreeing with Celeste. But he didn't feel that way now! Why had he changed so suddenly? It had to have something to do with Robert. She tried to remember her earlier conversation with him, but could find nothing in it to make Cesare so angry. And there could be no doubt in her mind that he had been angry.

'Then I'm glad I turned up.' Robert put a protective arm about her shoulders. 'Suzanne doesn't get into relationships like that, do you, love? Not even with Venetian counts.'

Suzanne too felt glad that Robert had 'turned up' later that evening, when Cesare arrived at the dinner accompanied by the exquisite Elena. The other girl looked beautiful, and she felt glad that she had dressed with care for this evening at a well-known but exclusive restaurant in the centre of town.

The gown she wore was new, an impulsive gift from Celeste a couple of days earlier. She had always wanted a Grecian styled gown, but never having much money it had been an impossibility. This gown was a deep rose colour, and Grecian as she had wanted. This gown was much more daring than anything she had ever worn before, caught in at the shoulders it smoothed down in two separate folds over her full breasts, and gathered together at the wide waistband to fall in clinging folds to her ankles. It was a beautiful gown and she hoped she could do it justice.

Robert appeared to think so and she felt more confi-

dent for his praise. Cesare and Elena were already
seated when the four of them arrived at eight-thirty,
although Cesare stood up politely at their entrance.
The introductions duly made Suzanne found herself
seated next to Cesare, Robert on her other side, and
she felt sure Celeste had engineered this. She looked
at her stepmother and saw her give a conspiratorial
wink. She *had* planned it!

She looked at Cesare uncertainly, hoping he hadn't
noticed Celeste's mischievous gesture. Love had certainly changed Celeste, and Vidal seemed equally be-
sotted, although it still seemed all to have happened
rather quickly. But they were both adults and had
known each other as long as she had known Cesare, and
she loved him! That was indisputable.

They were seated at a round table and this made
conversation easier. Elena Lindsay sat forward, a smile
on her perfectly curved lips. 'You're training to be a
teacher, I hear, Miss Hammond?'

It had come as something of a shock to learn that
this woman was English. But why not? Being half
English himself Cesare must have some relatives of that
nationality. 'Suzanne, please,' she answered softly, completely aware of Cesare as he sat silently between them.
Besides their first cursory greeting he had ignored her
completely. 'I'm at college and hope eventually to go
on to teacher training college, although whether I'll
actually make it to being a fully trained teacher I have
no idea.'

'You have doubts?' This, surprisingly, from Cesare,
as he watched her beneath lowered lids.

'I—— Well, I——' She shrugged her shoulders helplessly. 'Who's to know what will happen tomorrow?'
she laughed shakily.

'Who indeed?' he replied coldly.

'Perhaps you'll marry,' Elena continued, looking
suggestively at Robert.

Suzanne didn't miss that look. She shook her head emphatically. 'I doubt it.'

Cesare too looked at Robert as he chatted to Vidal. 'You could be right,' he drawled. 'One cannot choose where one loves,' he said distantly.

'No—no indeed.' Again that insinuation about Robert not being suitable for her to love. She frowned. Where on earth had he got that impression? If only she could work out what they had said to make his mood change so drastically from his earlier meeting with Celeste to when he had seen her at the hotel after seeing Robert and herself. Unless of course he just didn't like Robert being here, which was highly probable.

But he had only to ask her and she could have told him Robert was a friend and no more than that. But he hadn't asked and she couldn't just blurt it out. Look at the last time she had tried to put him right about jumping to conclusions; he just hadn't believed her. And he wouldn't be any different this time. She knew by the tightness of his jaw and the hardness of those flinty eyes.

He pointedly ignored her during the rest of the meal —at least, it seemed pointed to her; she doubted if anyone else noticed. Celeste and Vidal were totally engrossed with each other and the love they had surprisingly discovered for each other. In fact Vidal still looked dazed with the newness of the emotions he felt towards this sophisticated woman. Elena seemed intent on talking only to Cesare and as Robert seemed to feel the same way about their own conversation there was little chance for her to talk to Cesare, even fleetingly.

After the meal they all decided to go on to a nightclub, Cesare finding them a secluded corner. It was just after this that Celeste insisted they all dance, choosing Robert as her partner. Again that conspiratorial wink, and she realised why a few minutes later when

Cesare asked her to dance. He had little choice really, and she knew he had only done it out of politeness after Vidal had asked Elena.

She couldn't relax in his arms, her body stiff and unyielding. He was so distant from her, so aloof, that he didn't seem at all like the man who had held her passionately in his arms but a few short weeks ago.

He looked down at her. 'You are upset about Vidal's change of loyalties.'

It was a statement, not a question, but nevertheless Suzanne denied it hotly. 'Vidal is quite at liberty to escort whom he pleases.' She would have liked to have said more, but Celeste had sworn Robert and herself to secrecy about her marriage plans. It seemed Vidal hadn't yet told his brother and until he had it was not for public discussion.

'But you now feel neglected. Is that why you welcome the arms of your past lover so easily?' he demanded harshly.

Suzanne stood back in his arms. 'I won't pretend to know what you're talking about.'

'Robert Thompson.'

'Robert?' she frowned. 'He's a friend, nothing more than that.'

'Do you deny he is the married man you had an affair with?'

'I deny both counts.'

'Both?' Cesare looked puzzled. 'I do not understand.'

'Robert isn't married, and I've certainly never had an affair with him.'

'You do not have to pretend with me, Suzanne, I know how much you liked Vidal. I admit I did not approve of your association with him, and would have done anything to stop it, but I did not expect him to then take up with your stepmother.'

To Suzanne only one part of what he had said seemed important. 'You—you would have done anything to part Vidal and myself?' she repeated huskily. 'Does anything include pretending an interest in me yourself so that Vidal would believe me to have now transferred my interest to you, the richer and also titled brother?'

CHAPTER EIGHT

'Is that what you think?'

Suzanne remembered his complete control on the day of their picnic and knew it to be true, that he had only been pretending an interest in her as an inducement to Vidal to stop seeing her himself. And it had worked! Anger boiled up within her, hot boiling anger that gave her cheeks the warmth they had lacked of late, and gave life to her sparkling green eyes.

'Yes,' she replied sharply. 'Yes, that's exactly what I think! What a pity you didn't quite succeed—Vidal changing his interest to Celeste didn't enter your head at all, did it? Well, I'm glad it's happened,' she whispered vehemently. 'You think you're so clever, so omnipotent! Well, you're not! You can't always direct people's lives in the direction *you* think they should go. I'm glad Vidal's defied you, really glad!'

'I understand that you are upset and I——'

'I'm not *upset*, Cesare,' she laughed. 'I just find it rather sickening that you should try to deceive me this way. I never for one moment imagined your desire for me was anything *but* desire, but I certainly didn't expect you to have improvised even that.'

Cesare was angry too now, his eyes glacial. 'You go too far, Suzanne!'

Again she laughed, past caring where he was concerned. 'Oh no, Cesare, you did the first time you kissed me.' How could she act like this when inside she felt as if she were bruised so badly she might never recover? 'But then you're an expert, aren't you, practised in all the arts of lovemaking. Vidal warned me you were made out of pure granite, I should have listened to him.'

'You discussed me with Vidal?' His mouth was tight.

'Oh no, I didn't do that. That little snippet of information was just given in passing.' She pulled out of his arms. 'I believe I have something that belongs to you, I'll return it tomorrow, I don't have it with me.'

He frowned deeply. 'Something that belongs to me? I do not understand.'

'Don't you? Then let me tell you. I don't accept expensive gifts from any man, and that wristwatch certainly comes under that category. What did you think, Cesare, that I would be bought off, that I would get out of Vidal's life for a few gifts from you?' Her voice had risen shrilly, but she didn't care any more. 'When Vidal described you to me he didn't go quite far enough—you're a cold, unfeeling, arrogant brute, and I want nothing more to do with you! Excuse me.'

She turned on her heel and made her way back to their table, making her excuses to leave, much to the annoyance of Celeste, who was enjoying herself immensely, mainly at Suzanne's expense. 'It's early yet,' she insisted.

'We have to leave,' Suzanne said firmly. 'Robert's taking me to meet some of his friends at a discotheque.'

'But surely he can meet them another night,' Celeste frowned.

'No, it has to be tonight. Robert's only down for a couple of days.' Poor Robert, he looked totally confused. As he had never been to London before she felt sure he was mystifyed as to her saying he had friends here, but he wisely kept quiet.

Cesare had become seated again by this time, watching them through enigmatic eyes. 'If they have to leave, Celeste, they are perfectly at liberty to do so. They are probably bored by our company——'

'Oh, no——'

'They want to be with people their own age,' he continued.

Her denial died on her lips. Cesàre had just effectively reduced her to the role of the immature teenager
he no doubt considered her to be, so why should she
argue with him. 'Are you ready to leave, Robert?'

He gulped down the last of his whisky before standing to his feet. 'Ready,' he agreed.

Their goodbyes made they quickly made their way to
the exit, Suzanne breathing a sigh of relief as they came
out on to the street. She held her black velvet jacket
against her body, the evenings could still be quite cool
even though it was early summer.

'That was a bit sudden, wasn't it?' Robert matched
his steps to her shorter ones.

'What? Oh, sorry. Yes—yes, it was. That man has a
way of making even the largest of places seem too small
to contain both of us,' she muttered moodily.

'That man . . .? Oh, the Conte,' he nodded his understanding. 'Bit overpowering, isn't he, almost too much
to believe.'

Suzanne grinned. 'That's him exactly! Too damned
much of everything.'

'But especially sex appeal, hmm?' He eyed her curiously.

'That too,' she agreed. 'Oh, Robert, what am I going
to do?' It was a cry from the heart.

'You love him, don't you?'

'How did you——?' she sighed. 'It's obvious, I suppose.'

'No,' he shook his head. 'No, it isn't that. You just
aren't the same Suzanne that left Manchester three
weeks ago. You're all grown up somehow. I had hoped
I could be the one to make you feel like this, but I
know a better man when I see him,' he admitted ruefully.

Suzanne put out a hand to touch his arm. 'He isn't
a better man than you, Robert. You aren't cruel, and
cold, and bitingly sarcastic like he is. I can't understand

why I feel this way about him, he isn't at all what I expected the man I fell in love with to look like. And he treats me as a child,' she added disgustedly.

'That isn't the impression dear Celeste gave, or the one I received myself. A child hardly describes how he regards you.'

The two of them were walking slowly beside the river, the bright lights of the city reflected in amazing beauty. There was quite a breeze blowing across the water and she shivered slightly before wrapping her jacket more tightly about her. 'I didn't say that he doesn't find me attractive, but he also finds me juvenile. You've seen the way he treats me—hardly polite, is it?'

'Hardly *im*polite either, I don't think he could ever be that. No, I agree with Celeste, he's definitely interested in you. I didn't like the way he looked at you at all.'

She threaded her arm through his. 'He's only ever looked, Robert.'

'Oh, I realise that, you haven't changed that much. Where does the beautiful Elena come into the scene? Is she his fiancée or just a friend?'

'She's his cousin, actually, although I think she wishes it was more than that,' she said dryly.

'I think you're right,' he grinned. 'Look, how about if we really do go on to a disco, we could have fun, discuss the crowd back home? Like, did you know Eddie and Kay have got engaged?'

'No!' she cried excitedly. 'Tell me about it.'

In the end they didn't go to a disco but to a coffee bar, their conversation taking them into the early hours of the morning. Suzanne enjoyed the way she could relax in Robert's company, it was such a change after the last few weeks. They laughed and joked together as if nothing had changed between them, and in a way nothing had, she had always regarded him as nothing more than a very dear friend.

They parted at the hotel with an agreement to meet for lunch the next day. 'And don't worry about the Count, Suzanne,' Robert reassured her. 'Things will work out.'

Back in her room Suzanne wished he hadn't mentioned Cesare again this evening—or rather, morning. She stretched, yawning. Goodness, she was tired. It had been a long day, a long, long day.

'So Vidal still hasn't told his brother?' Suzanne confirmed.

'No.' Celeste pulled another dress off the rack, turning it from side to side before deciding she didn't like it. She wrinkled her nose. 'When Vidal and I are married I intend having all my clothes specially made for me, none of this making do.'

Suzanne would have liked to point out that Celeste had never 'made do', but didn't think it worth the ensuing argument. 'And how soon is the wedding to be?'

'Oh, I don't know,' Celeste replied carelessly. 'We don't need Cesare's permission, you know.'

'I know that, but——'

'Don't fuss, Suzanne.' She picked up a lime green silk scarf, holding it against her. 'How does this look with my hair?'

'Fine,' Suzanne replied distractedly. 'Couldn't you stop looking at those clothes for a moment and talk to me sensibly?'

'I asked you to come out shopping with me, not to have sensible conversations. I can sort out my own life, thank you, I've managed to up until now and I should think I'll continue to do so. Vidal isn't the strongest of men.'

'But Cesare told me that Vidal——'

'Supposedly has a fiancée in Venice,' Celeste finished

for her. 'He told me the same thing. Unfortunately for him I couldn't give a damn about this so-called fiancée, and apparently neither can Vidal.'

'Cesare isn't going to like it. He warned me quite strongly.'

Celeste shrugged. 'So what can he do? Vidal has his own money, he isn't dependent on Cesare for anything, not even his job, the company is a family concern.'

'But Cesare——'

'Oh, damn Cesare!' Celeste snapped angrily. 'Will you stop saying Cesare said this and Cesare said that! You're beginning to sound like Vidal. Cesare isn't omnipotent, you know.'

'He just gives that impression,' Suzanne returned dryly.

Celeste shrugged. 'So what? Vidal will tell him about us in his own good time, I'm leaving it completely up to him.'

'Does he know——' Suzanne began again. 'Does Vidal know that you—*we* don't have any money?'

Celeste smiled. 'He knows,' she confirmed. 'I told you, Suzanne, this hasn't happened at all the way I planned it,' she dismissed the assistant who was heading in their direction. 'Falling in love with Vidal wasn't part of my plan. Of course he knows I'm broke, but it doesn't make any difference. He wasn't fooled by my rich widow routine, and apparently neither was Cesare.'

'Are you saying Vidal doesn't mind?'

'Why should he? He has enough money not to need any more. We're going house hunting this afternoon,' she exclaimed excitedly.

Suzanne raised her eyebrows. 'You intend living in London?'

'Not London, but somewhere very near. Vidal will still have to travel into work each day.'

This new unselfish Celeste was quite a surprise after her usual behaviour. Not that she minded this new

Celeste, she just hoped it was going to last. There could be no doubt that she was in love, it was there in her glowing blue eyes and the constant curve to her painted lips.

'Cesare will be returning to Venice quite soon,' Celeste continued. 'Vidal has to tell him about our forthcoming marriage before then or it will be too late.'

She continued to chatter on, and in her excitement didn't notice Suzanne's monosyllabic replies. Cesare would be returning home soon! And when that happened she wouldn't see him again. She was so quiet during lunch that eventually Robert had to say something.

'What's happened?' He grinned. 'Is Celeste back to her old obnoxious self?'

Suzanne's answering smile didn't quite reach her shadowed eyes. 'Not yet. I suppose love can change some people.' It had certainly changed her, and not for the better; she felt so miserable it was unbelievable.

'I think the younger Martino will handle her just as well as the Conte would have done. With his brother he may be a little weak, who wouldn't, but with a woman I should think it's a completely different story. He's a fine specimen, isn't he?'

'If you say so.' Vidal still wasn't her favourite person, in fact she felt Celeste and Vidal deserved each other.

'I thought you went out with him first?' he probed.

'Only once or twice. What are we going to do this afternoon?'

'Changing the subject? Oh well, I suppose we've discussed the Martinos enough. Oh, except—well, I met the Conte earlier, he was acting very strangely,' he frowned.

'Strangely?'

'Mmm, peculiar looks, things like that. I had the feeling he heartily dislikes me.'

'I'm sure you're wrong,' she shook her head. 'It's me he dislikes. He thinks I'm after a man, any man.'

Robert burst out laughing, signalling the waiter to bring their bill. They had chosen to eat at a restaurant in town, leaving the exclusive part of London where the hotel was situated, and walking until they found a restaurant they liked. It was in a quiet side street and wasn't too crowded.

'You've got to be kidding,' he chuckled. '*You*, a man-chaser? It took me months to get you to even have coffee with me. There's only one man-chaser in your family, and we both know who that is.'

They spent the afternoon window-shopping, parting quite early as Suzanne was feeling rather tired after her late night the previous evening. She was in bed by ten o'clock, tossing about restlessly in covers that seemed far too hot and heavy. By twelve o'clock she was up and dressed again, deciding to take a stroll in the garden, at least it was cool outside. Actually it was cool inside, it was just that she wasn't in the mood for sleep. Where was Cesare?—she hadn't seen him all day. For all she knew he might have already left for Venice. But no, Robert said he had seen him earlier, so he couldn't have gone yet.

The hotel was deserted at this time of night, except for a few meagre night staff, so she slipped quietly out of the side door. It was curiously quiet in the garden, although she felt sure that in the centre of town a mile or two away there would be plenty of people and traffic, and noise that she couldn't stand at the moment.

'Who are you sneaking off so stealthily to meet?' demanded a taut voice. 'Your married lover, or could it be my gullible brother?'

Suzanne swung round. 'Do you have to keep creeping up on me like that?'

He looked very remote and she blanched at the contempt in his face. 'Answer the question, Suzanne.'

She turned away uninterestedly. 'I'm not sneaking off to meet anyone. I came out for some air.'

'At twelve o'clock at night?'

'Why not? It seems as good a time as any, especially when you can't sleep.'

Cesare moved closer to her, his dinner jacket gleaming whitely in the darkness. 'And why can you not sleep?'

'I'm too hot,' she mumbled.

'Your room is air-conditioned, all the rooms are.'

'I didn't say the room was hot, only me.'

'Feverish thoughts of one of your lover's?' he taunted.

Suzanne just wasn't in the mood for his barbed comments at the moment and she turned on him angrily. 'You're letting your imagination run wild!' she said savagely. 'Or else you know something I don't.'

'I know your body responds to caresses like a finely tuned instrument,' he drawled, moving forward and smiling slightly as she stepped back. 'It does not appear to be the reaction of a novice. I am sure that while I was away you found someone else to entertain you. And of course you now have Robert. God, you must really be something for him to abandon his wife and run down here at your bidding!'

'It wasn't my bidding,' she denied impatiently. 'Celeste asked him to come here.'

'But only because of your condition,' he snapped. 'You have deteriorated since I last saw you, you have lost weight, you do not appear to sleep. This Robert loves you as much as you appear to love him, so why does he not leave his wife?'

'Would you—in the same circumstances?'

'I do not know,' he admitted bitterly.

She knew this was some admission coming from a Venetian, who upheld the marriage vows at all costs. 'You—you don't know?' she repeated.

Cesare moved away impatiently. 'No,' he agreed tautly, 'I do not know. You have my permission to laugh if you wish.'

She gave a broken sound that was nothing like a laugh. 'Why should I laugh?' she said softly.

'No,' he smiled sardonically. 'You have little to laugh about, do you? How do you think it will end, Suzanne? Will you continue all your life with this helpless passion for a married man, always on the outside of his life but unable to give him up?'

'You're so wrong about Robert and me, Cesare. I don't love him and he isn't married. I don't know why you should think he is. Celeste was just being spiteful when she made that comment about my having an affair with a married man. It wasn't true.'

'I want you so badly myself, *cara*, that I cannot think straight. You can have no conception of how I feel just looking at you. And you are wasting it all on *him*!' he finished with disgust.

Her eyes searched his face avidly. 'What do you mean, Cesare? How do you feel about me?'

'I desire you. You returned my gift to me and I thought I did not stand a chance with you. But that cannot be, you must also feel desire for me or you would not have responded in my arms as you have done on a number of occasions. As I could make you do now,' he added dangerously.

'Could you, Cesare?' she enticed him softly, longing only to be in his arms.

'Yes!' he said savagely. 'But I do not want you to hate me any more than you do now.'

'I won't hate you, Cesare.'

'Oh *God*! Come here ...' Strong hands grasped her, pulling her roughly against his taut roused body. 'You have invited this,' he groaned against her mouth. 'Remember that.'

She didn't want to remember anything, she only

wanted to feel, to revel in the slumbering sensuality of this man. But it didn't slumber for long; his hands were doing strange things to her as they roamed expertly over her body. His lips teased and cajoled, making her almost beg for more than those feather-light caresses on her lips.

Finally his mouth parted hers to explore further and his hands were assured against her naked back as they freely caressed her fevered skin. Their thighs and hips were moulded together as they fused in action and he moved against her in slow drugging movements.

His hands moved up over her breasts to cradle each side of her face, moving his lips slowly back and forth across her mouth until she stood on tiptoe and put her hands behind his head to increase the pressure of those pleasure-giving caresses.

'Cesare,' she sighed. 'Oh, Cesare ...'

'Do not speak, *cara*,' he replied huskily. 'Just love.'

Their breathing was ragged and laboured and Suzanne knew that she could never respond to someone else with this abandonment, with this feeling that what she was doing was completely right for her. And there could be no doubt that she had invited this, had asked for these long languorous kisses, had deliberately and sensually aroused him until he could not refuse the invitation of her body.

And he was not refusing, touching her bare skin beneath the thin vest-top that was all the clothing she had on besides her denims. A bra hadn't seemed necessary when she was only going out into the garden for a few minutes, and Cesare was soon aware of this fact, those long sensitive fingers soon bringing her breasts to full pulsating life.

'Your body is beautiful, Suzanne,' he moaned against her. 'Perfect and glorious.'

'Cesare, I——'

He stopped her words with his firm mouth. 'I do not

want you to talk, only listen. You have skin as soft as a rose petal, a figure of Venus, beautiful drowning eyes, hair the colour of sunlight. You are——' he seemed at a loss for words. 'You are infinitely desirable, my darling.'

'So are you,' she admitted.

He gave a low sound of triumph before claiming her lips once more. She thought she would die from the pleasure she was receiving from those expert hands, although her own hands had not been idle. The buttons on the front of his white silk shirt were now all undone to reveal the dark hairs on his chest, and her hands and arms were inside the shirt against his warm skin. She could feel the ripple of muscle at his movements and revelled in his power, just loving the feel of him.

She felt bereft when he removed his lips once more, but did not move his body too, resting his chin lightly on top of her head. 'You can feel what you do to me,' he said huskily. 'Feel the power this body of yours has over me. And you feel the same way about me. When I received back your gift I did not think that was possible.'

Neither had the receptionist. It had been the same girl who had handed her the gift and she had so obviously returned the same gift with just a message to give it to Conte Martino. Obviously she had done so.

'I couldn't accept it from you,' she told him softly.

'Not then perhaps, but now.' His lips travelled from her earlobe slowly over to her mouth, tantalising her lips apart to ravish the sweetness within. 'Mmm, that is good, so good.'

She nuzzled into his neck, loving the clean male smell of him and the tantalising roughness of his skin. 'I could never accept something as valuable as that obviously was.'

'Not even if you become my mistress as I once asked

you to be?' He carried on, not noticing the sudden stiff-
ness of her body as she started to draw away from him.
'You will come back to Venice with me and I will set
you up in a house that is conveniently near to the
Palazzo and yet not near enough for you to feel any embarrassment.'

'I——' Suzanne licked her suddenly dry lips, search-
ing his face for some sign of teasing and finding none.
He was actually serious! 'Wh-what do you mean,
Cesare?'

He laughed exultantly. 'I want you to come back to
Venice with me. I want to possess you, utterly and completely. You will love my country, it is old and sinking
but has a grandeur of beauty not to be equalled. I will
take you to the Piazza San Marco, to the Basilica,
places all tourists love to see. And I will take you to the
Lido—you will love the Lido, it is beautiful there and
you can swim if you want to. Perhaps then you will
gain some of the colour you have lost.'

She had lost even more during the last few minutes,
her cheeks so deathly white that her eyes appeared like
huge green pools. 'I——'

'You have been ill, I know. But I will help you to
get better.'

She pulled away from him. 'I can't do what you ask,
Cesare, I can't!'

Cesare grasped her arms, forcing her to look at him.
'I understand, Suzanne. Oh God, how I understand!
But I can make you forget him. In my arms you
will——'

She shook off his hold, her happiness of a few
moments ago turning to a living hell. 'Forget who,
Cesare? What are you talking about?'

He ran a hand through his light-coloured hair. 'Robert Thompson. I will make you forget how it feels to
be in his arms, how his caresses arouse you. You will
think only of me and the exciting things we will do

together, the places we will go.'

'As long as it doesn't cause a scandal!' she suggested shrilly.

'That is as much for your sake as mine.'

'You're old-fashioned, Cesare,' she said bitterly. 'Lots of men keep *lady friends* nowadays.'

'Like Robert Thompson has you? God, you have no idea how much I hate the thought of him touching one inch of you.' He smiled with effort. 'But I will put that to the back of my mind. Will you not come with me? You will never have to want for anything again, not anything.'

'For how long? Until you tire of me? Until you find someone else you *desire*?'

'Suzanne!' he looked shocked. 'What are you saying?'

'No!'

'But why?' His eyes darkened angrily. 'You cannot have this Robert, he must always go back to his wife.'

'As you will once you marry.' She glared at him. 'I happen to be slightly old-fashioned about these things myself—I believe in marriage.'

Cesare's face became a shuttered mask and he visibly withdrew from her, both physically and mentally. 'I do not believe I mentioned marriage.'

'No, you didn't,' she agreed. 'I'm not asking *you* for marriage, Cesare, I'm not asking you for anything. I suppose I should feel flattered that you even desire me, but somehow I don't feel anything but disgust. You have the wrong idea about my morals, the wrong idea completely.'

'Think it over, Suzanne. Do not be too hasty in your decision. We could be happy together.'

She shook her head. 'It's not for me.'

'You prefer to be Robert Thompson's plaything? My God, what do you see in him! What does his wife think of all this? Does she know about you?'

'For the last time, Robert has no wife!' she told him savagely, hardly able to believe that a few short minutes ago they had been trembling passionately in each other's arms. 'I don't know where you gained such an erroneous impression.'

'I heard it from his own lips.'

'I don't believe it!' Robert wouldn't tell such a lie. He had accepted that she didn't love him and he was too much of a friend to want to hurt her, Cesare must have misunderstood something that had been said. She only wished she knew what it was.

Cesare shrugged. 'Believe what you want, I only know what I have heard. So you will not come with me?'

'No.'

'Then I will leave you to get this fresh air you say you are in need of. I am sorry if I have offended you in any way.'

'You haven't. I suppose I always knew you would suggest something like that. I even invited it.'

'Goodnight.'

'Goodnight,' she echoed huskily.

'What do you mean, you're leaving?' Celeste demanded. 'You can't just walk out on me like this!'

The two of them were lingering over lunch, although neither of them seemed to have much of an appetite. 'I'm not walking out on you, Celeste, I'm merely going home.' Suzanne had come to this decision during the long hours she had lain awake during the night, long hours when she could think of little but Cesare.

Celeste's mouth tightened. 'I won't let you do it.'

'Don't be silly. You don't need me here, you have Vidal.'

'Vidal and I have argued.'

'You—you've *what*? But why?' She was genuinely

upset for Celeste, believing that she and Vidal would be happy together.

Celeste shrugged casually, but Suzanne could tell she was more worried by this argument than she cared to admit. 'I should have realised it had all happened too quickly. I'm not usually so impulsive. But anyway, it's over now.'

'Over? But—but it can't be! What happened?'

'Oh, he told Cesare this morning that we intended marrying, and apparently the haughty Conte flipped his lid. He really laid down the law, said it was too soon, that Vidal was making a mistake thinking of marrying someone like me.'

'So? You expected a certain amount of opposition.'

'Of course I did, but I didn't expect Vidal to baulk at the first hurdle,' Celeste said in disgust. 'I don't want to marry someone who can't even stand up to his own brother.'

'I wouldn't have thought Cesare's approval would have mattered to Vidal, he doesn't seem to like him very much.'

'That's all a front. He actually admires his brother very much. Hating him has just become a habit with him.'

'It didn't sound that way when he spoke to me.'

'Well, it is. So, I've called a halt to the marriage plans.'

'But you can't really mean it, Celeste. I've seen the two of you together. You love him, I know you do.'

A flicker of pain crossed Celeste's face before it was quickly masked. 'Love!' she scoffed. 'I let it cloud my judgment for a while, but it won't happen again.'

'I don't believe you. You can't just turn off love because it doesn't quite work out the way you want it to.' Suzanne should know, she still loved Cesare even after all the things he had accused her of, and his insulting offer.

'I can,' Celeste vowed. 'How do you think I survived the last few years? Well, I'll tell you. I did it by turning off all emotion.' She gave a bitter laugh. 'I must have gone overboard when I finally allowed myself to feel. I don't love Vidal, it's just infatuation. He's fun and I enjoy being with him. That's all it was, all it ever could be.'

Suzanne knew Celeste was kidding herself, telling herself it was so because she didn't want to get hurt. Poor Celeste! But who could blame her? Certainly not she; she knew what the pain of loving someone could be like, it was almost unbearable. Better to let Celeste believe what she was saying, although she had the feeling that once on her own Celeste would break down.

'If you say so,' she agreed.

'I do,' Celeste answered firmly. 'So how are you making out? Have you seen Cesare lately?'

'I've seen him,' Suzanne admitted with a grimace. 'I think that's over too.'

'Was it my fault? I did try to explain to him, but——'

'He wouldn't listen to you,' Suzanne finished. 'I've tried to tell him too, but it makes no impression on him. He thinks Robert is the married man in my life.'

'Ridiculous! I can't imagine why he should think such a thing. He said as much to me. Robert!' Celeste made a face. 'Hardly the sort of man to inspire that sort of impetuous feeling, is he?'

'Now don't be nasty, Robert's a very nice boy.'

'Exactly. He's hardly old enough to be married, let alone be having an affair too. Cesare insisted that he heard Robert himself talking about his wife. I told him he was mistaken, but he said he even knew her name.'

'He does?' Suzanne raised surprised eyebrows.

'Mm, Patsy or something like that.'

'Patsy?' Suzanne squeaked. 'Did you say Patsy?'

'That's right. Is something wrong?'

Patsy! Cesare thought Patsy was Robert's wife! Oh, no, she couldn't believe it!

CHAPTER NINE

SHE would have laughed if she didn't feel quite so much like crying. Cesare thought Patsy, a harmless cat, was Robert's wife! He must have heard the two of them talking and come to completely the wrong conclusion.

'Suzanne! Will you answer me? What's wrong? Who is this Patsy?'

'Patsy is a cat,' she burst out.

'A *cat*!' Celeste shook her head. 'I don't believe you.'

'But she is.'

'How can she be? Cesare is convinced that this Patsy is Robert's wife.'

'Yes, and I know how he came to that conclusion. But I do assure you that Robert is not married and that Patsy is no more that a Siamese cat. It doesn't matter now, anyway. I know Cesare's interest in me, and it's no more than a physical thing.'

'I don't think so. Vidal said——'

'Now don't you start,' Suzanne interrupted. 'I don't want to hear what Vidal did or did not say.'

'No, you're right, I don't want to hear it either,' Celeste wrinkled her nose.

'I *am* leaving, Celeste,' Suzanne said firmly.

'This is ridiculous—you can't leave me now!'

Suzanne stood up. 'I'm not going to argue with you. I'm leaving with Robert when he goes today.'

Celeste's eyes became stormy. 'I won't let you go!'

'You won't stop me,' Suzanne said calmly before walking out of the dining-room. She only had a little of her packing left to do and a quick telephone call to

Robert to tell him she would be accompanying him back to Manchester.

Her mind was firmly made up. The previous evening she had spent hours trying to decide what would be the best thing for her to do. Her heart told her to accept what Cesare was prepared to give, but her mind logically told her that this was the wrong thing to do.

Despite stating that she was an old-fashioned girl who believed in marriage she wasn't sure that she could stand another face-to-face encounter with Cesare. She would probably launch herself into his arms and agree to anything he suggested.

So she thought it best to remove herself from temptation. There was a chance that Cesare would be returning to Venice in the near future, but it wasn't a certainty. So it was up to her to leave. It wasn't as if she could easily avoid seeing him; he was also staying at this hotel and so used the same dining-room as Celeste and herself.

'Hello, love,' Robert greeted her with a grin.

'Robert!' she smiled at him. 'This saves me the trouble of calling you.'

He raised a querying eyebrow once he heard of her plans. 'Running away?' he suggested gently.

'Certainly not! I——' she broke off at the look on his face. 'Well, perhaps I am. But what else would you have me do? Go back to Venice with him and be kept in luxury, but also be hidden from respectable eyes? I don't think so, thank you, Robert.'

'Maybe you're right. I don't——'

'Suzanne!' Vidal came into reception, not looking at all his usual self. His hair was windswept and disarranged, and he didn't look at all sure of himself.

Suzanne hadn't really spoken to him since she had learnt of his wedding plans. This hadn't been intentional, she had just been too wrapped up in her own feelings for Cesare to indulge in casual conversation with the man she had once thought to love.

How immature she had been to think that just because Vidal looked as she had imagined her dream man to look that she would immediately fall in love with him. Oh, she had to admit that she had been very attracted to him, but one kiss from Cesare had put an end to all that.

In Cesare's arms she came alive, her body aflame with pure longing and desire. Now it was as if any time not spent feeling wonderfully aware of Cesare and his beautifully compelling hands was just time wasted.

Well, it looked as if she was going to be doing that a lot in future. 'You look upset, Vidal,' she said.

'Of course I am upset,' he said in disgust. 'Celeste has called off the wedding and now will not even speak to me.'

'Surely that was only to be expected, Vidal. When you can put Cesare before your own fiancée you have to expect trouble.'

'But I did not——' He glared ferociously at Robert. 'I would appreciate it if we did not discuss my personal affairs in such a public place.'

Robert cursed himself for allowing this man's damned arrogance to get under his skin. Arrogance seemed to be something the Martinos possessed in abundance. 'Don't mind me,' he said stiffly. 'I was just leaving.'

'No, you weren't,' Suzanne denied. 'We were in the middle of a personal conversation ourselves. You certainly don't have to leave, Robert. We have our arrangements to make.'

Robert didn't at all like the looks he was receiving from the older man. 'They're quite simple, Suzanne. We have to get the four o'clock train, so I'll call for you at three-thirty.'

'Are you sure?'

He knew she referred to him leaving now. 'I'm sure,' he confirmed.

'Okay then, I'll see you later.' Once he had left she turned angrily on Vidal. 'Now that you've quite finished insulting my friend perhaps you would like to start on me?'

Vidal sighed impatiently. 'I did not mean to be rude to your friend. I am not myself today. Celeste refusing to speak to me has confused and upset all my plans.'

'Upset all *your* plans? How do you think Celeste feels? She was all set to marry you and you've let her down.'

He took a firm hold of her arm. 'Let us go out into the garden where we will not be disturbed.'

Suzanne reluctantly went along with him, speaking again once they were seated. 'What do we have to talk about, Vidal? You've changed your mind about marrying Celeste because your brother doesn't approve. Forgive me if all my sympathies lie with her and not with you.'

'But you are wrong, Suzanne. I have not changed my mind at all.' He patted his breast pocket. 'I have the licence for my marriage to Celeste right here, I have done for several days now.'

She frowned her puzzlement. 'But Celeste said you'd told her Cesare doesn't approve.'

'He does not. But that does not worry me. I am adult enough to make my own decisions concerning my own wife.'

'Then if I were you I would tell Celeste that straight away. And don't listen to any arguments, just rush her off her feet and don't give her time to think. You know how stubborn she can be.'

He gave a rueful grin. 'I am learning. Oh, how I am learning!'

'Well, go on, then. Celeste was in the dining-room five minutes ago, she can't have got far.'

'First I must speak to you. Your friend Robert said you were leaving. Where are you going?'

'Home.'

'Does Cesare know of this?'

'Cesare? Why should he know?' Her question came out casually enough, but that wasn't how she felt. Cesare's name only had to be mentioned and she felt a trembling mass of nerves.

'But you and Cesare are—— Well, you are——' he sought in his mind for the right word.

'I can guess what you're trying to say, Vidal—and you would be completely wrong. Cesare and I aren't *anything*. I don't know where you gained the impression that we were.' Suzanne successfully evaded his searching eyes.

'From Cesare himself, of course. Do you know the reason he disapproved of my marriage to Celeste? It was because of you.'

'Me?' She was astounded. Surely Cesare didn't hate her enough to include Celeste in his displeasure? 'What have I done?'

'Apparently you have told Cesare that you do not love this Robert Thompson, and so he has concluded you are in love with me. I have told him that he is mistaken, but he insists that your wan appearance can be due to nothing else.'

'How ridiculous! Why should I have to be in love with anyone? You men are so conceited,' she said crossly.

'Then you are not in love with me?'

'Certainly not!' she answered angrily.

'I did not think you were. Once Cesare came on the scene I knew I did not stand a chance with you. That was why it was so easy for Celeste and me to become friends—and fall in love. I do not usually drop one woman so callously in favour of another, but I could see I had lost my charm as far as you were concerned.

And Celeste and I seem to have so much in common...'

'You don't have to sound apologetic, Vidal. As you've said, we're not suited at all. I don't love anyone. So you can safely marry Celeste with a clear conscience.'

'You are not telling the truth, Suzanne,' he shook his head. 'You are in love, I can see that. I can also see who you are in love with. Cesare must be a fool not to see it.'

'You're mistaken,' she denied vehemently. It was bad enough admitting it to herself, without everyone else realising it.

Again he shook his head. 'I am not. And he loves you too.'

She looked at him sharply. 'That isn't true. I don't love him and he doesn't love me. I admit we're attracted to each other, but that's all.'

'It is not all,' Vidal insisted. 'Why else should Cesare insist that my first duty lies with you? I will tell you why. His jealousy has led him to believe you are in love with me, and to feel jealousy he must be in love with you himself.'

'You're wrong, Vidal.'

'I do not think so. It is strange, is it not, that when you and I first met I said I would like to see Cesare bowed with love for a woman. I did not expect that woman to be you.'

'It isn't,' Suzanne told him impatiently.

'It is also strange, but I do not feel the elation I expected to,' he said slowly.

'That's quite simple to explain, Vidal. You don't hate your brother at all, you only thought you did.'

'I think perhaps you are right. I have always been rather in awe of him, perhaps because he had to take care of me when he was only twenty himself, and I resented it. It is not important now. What is important is that you see him before you leave.'

'No,' she said firmly. 'I don't think we have any more to say to one another. And I think you should go and see Celeste now.'

Vidal stood up. 'Perhaps you are right.' He stopped suddenly. 'Have you thought, Suzanne, I will be your stepfather when Celeste and I are married?' He gave a mischievous grin. 'I promise to try not to be too strict.'

'You won't be strict at all, because I doubt we'll meet very often. Celeste and I rarely meet.' And she certainly wasn't going to go anywhere where there might be the remotest possibility of her bumping into Cesare.

'Things will be different when we are married. As your only male relative I will be responsible for you.'

'Don't be silly, Vidal. We won't be even vaguely related.'

'In Venice we do not take these things so lightly. You will come and stay with us often.'

'I don't think Celeste will agree with you,' she told him with a smile. She and Celeste might have come to a better understanding of each other during the last few weeks, but she didn't think they would ever be that close.

Vidal held himself haughtily. 'Celeste and I have already discussed it.'

'You—you *have*?'

'Yes,' he replied stiffly. 'And we have agreed that during the vacation time you will stay with us. We will of course leave you to finish your education in Manchester, Celeste assures me this is perfectly correct, but for the holidays you must come to us.'

'Don't you think you should have asked me first before making all these plans for me?'

'It was not necessary. Celeste and I will be responsible for you.'

'Don't you think it's rather late in the day for Celeste to be feeling this way?'

'I know all about your life since Celeste married your

father, she has held nothing back from me. But Celeste realises she has been wrong, she wishes to make it up to you for all the hardship you have suffered because of her in the past.'

'Really?'

They both turned at the shrillness of that voice. Vidal moved forward, only to stop in his tracks at the look on Celeste's face. '*Cara?*' he prompted softly.

Her eyes flashed. 'Don't you "*cara*" me! It isn't two minutes since we decided not to marry after all and already you're chasing Suzanne again. I was right about you, Vidal. Thank goodness I found out about you before we were married!'

Vidal looked devastated. '*Cara!*' he said reproachfully.

Suzanne cut in before Celeste once again remonstrated him for using that endearment. 'Vidal and I were only talking, Celeste. As usual you're jumping to conclusions. Vidal came here to talk to you, apparently you didn't let him finish his conversation earlier. Your wedding plans aren't cancelled at all. Now will you let him talk to you?'

'Vidal?' Celeste looked at him uncertainly.

'It is true, my love. The fact that Cesare has raised certain objections is not important. His reasoning was wrong anyway.'

'Excuse me,' interrupted Suzanne when it looked as if Celeste might launch herself into Vidal's waiting arms. 'I feel like an unwanted third. I wish you both the best of luck. 'Bye!'

She made her escape before they completely forgot her existence. They wouldn't even notice her absence for an hour or so, and with any luck by that time she would have packed and left the hotel altogether.

The journey back to Manchester had been quite uneventful, and Suzanne had felt relieved when they eventually reached the house where they both rented rooms. This had been where they first met, although their both being at college had strengthened their friendship.

Patsy was ecstatic about seeing Robert again, following him about wherever he went, her purrs loud and joyful. Suzanne couldn't help laughing at the drooling cat, which caused Patsy to stick her nose arrogantly in the air whenever she came near her. This caused her even more humour at Patsy's expense.

Oh, it was so good to be home, far away from Cesare's disruptive influence on her life. She would have liked to have seen him again before she left, but had found out from the desk that the Conte Martino was out for the day, presumably at his office. If he had continued asking her to go back to Venice with him she had a feeling she would have given in, so perhaps it was as well she hadn't seen him.

It didn't take her long to unpack the elegant clothing she had worn in London, although she had no idea when she would ever be anywhere smart enough to wear them again. They weren't exactly the sort of clothes she could wear to college. In fact it was quite a relief to be able to relax in denims and a vest top.

The door to her room stood open as usual, all the tenants in this house being college students and most of them friends. They wandered into each other's rooms quite freely, and Suzanne looked up and smiled as Robert walked in, followed closely by the loyal Patsy.

'The crowd are all going down to the coffee-bar in about an hour. Feel like going?' He sat down on the floor, which was his usual practice.

Suzanne put down the patchwork quilt she had been working on. 'I guess so, I haven't had anything to eat since lunchtime.'

'What a shame,' he teased. 'You must be almost starving to death!'

She looked down in exasperation as Patsy climbed

up on to the bed and sat herself down on the patch-work quilt, making a big show of cleaning herself. 'Look at this cat,' she said in disgust. 'Doesn't she realise that some of us have work to do?'

'She couldn't give a damn,' Robert chuckled. 'She does it to me all the time, especially when I'm trying to study.'

Patsy had finished washing now and was settling more comfortably on the quilt. Suzanne tickled her under the chin. 'You're spoilt, young lady,' she told her sternly.

'Isn't she just? So you think your dear stepmama and the younger Martino will definitely marry?' he asked, changing the subject.

'Yes,' she answered shortly. 'Do we have to talk about them?'

'Not if you don't want to.'

'I don't.' She looked up as Mrs Holmes came to the door; a woman in her mid-fifties, she was perhaps the nearest thing Suzanne had ever had to a mother. She was plump and homely and had mothered Suzanne from the day she had moved in here two years ago. 'Hello, love,' Suzanne smiled. 'I'm back from sin city,' she joked.

'So I can see.' Mrs Holmes looked harassed. 'And you already have a visitor.'

Suzanne raised a surprised eyebrow. Mrs Holmes didn't usually bring up the visitors herself. 'A visitor?' she repeated stupidly.

The man behind Mrs Holmes stepped forward and Suzanne gasped her surprise. Cesare! No wonder Mrs Holmes looked slightly overwhelmed. She shot off the bed, disturbing the sleeping cat and receiving a loud screech for her thoughtless action. Robert jumped up guiltily from his lounging position against the side of her bed, adding to the incongruousness of the circum-stance.

'Cesare,' she muttered softly.

Robert shifted uncomfortably under the piercing stare of the other man. 'Er—— We—— We'll see you later, Suzanne.' He scooped up the ruffled Patsy off the bed. 'Nice to see you again, Conte.'

The Conte merely nodded acknowledgment of having heard him at all, stepping into the room and closing the door firmly behind him. 'This is your room?' His voice was cold and clipped.

Suzanne ran nervous hands down her denims, sure that Cesare had never entered such a humble abode before. 'Yes,' she answered defensively. 'What do you want?'

'Well, I certainly did not want to find Robert Thompson in your bedroom.'

'Why not? You're in it yourself now. I only have the one room so it's difficult not to be.' She was being shrewish and she couldn't stop herself. What was he doing here? Goodness, she had only left London a few hours ago herself, he must have driven straight here when he found out she had left. But why?

Cesare moved further into the room, unbuttoning the jacket of his lightweight suit. Goodness, he was handsome! 'Why was Thompson here?'

'I'm sure you can answer that for yourself,' she said tartly.

'I could, but I would not necessarily be correct. Why was he here?' There was an inflexibility about his mouth that demanded she answer.

Suzanne shrugged. 'He lives here,' she told him truthfully.

'With you?'

'No, not with me! He has a room on the next floor.'

'And his wife?'

'Will you get it into your head that Robert is not married!'

'And Patsy? Explain her.'

'You just met her,' she said impatiently. 'She was the one with four legs and covered in fur.'

'A cat?' he asked sharply. 'Are you trying to tell me Patsy is a cat?'

'I'm not just telling you, I'm almost screaming it at you! If you don't believe me just ask Robert. Or even Patsy herself—she'd soon let you know that she answers to her name. Is that what you came here for, to question me again?'

'I would hardly drive all this way just to ask you a few questions. You do realise that Vidal and Celeste are going to be married?'

He was prowling about like a caged lion, making her room seem smaller and shabbier than usual. 'Yes, I realise that.'

'Is that why you left?'

'Look, Cesare, considering you said you didn't drive all this way to ask me questions you're doing an awful lot of it.' Suzanne attempted a light laugh. 'And no, that isn't why I left. I knew a few days ago that they intended getting married, I would have left then if it had bothered me. You could have asked me how I felt about Vidal before assuming I was in love with him. He told me about your refusing to accept Celeste as his future wife.'

'I have changed my mind. That is why I am here. They are getting married tomorrow. You will naturally wish to be there. If you had seen Celeste before leaving she could have explained all this to you.'

'I had already told her I was leaving.'

'So I believe.'

'I left her a note explaining,' she defended herself.

'I know that also. Would you like to collect a few things together and we will be on our way.'

Suzanne looked puzzled. 'On our way where?'

'Back to London. I have come to collect you and take you back for the wedding tomorrow.'

'I could have come on the train.'

'You would not have known,' he said haughtily. 'I believe this house does not have a telephone.'

'There is such a thing as a telegram,' she replied tartly.

'Do not be so stubborn all the time, Suzanne. I am here now. If you can be ready to leave in ten minutes or so?'

'I suppose so,' she answered ungraciously. 'Although it seems slightly ridiculous to be returning to London so soon after leaving. I've only been home a few hours.'

'That is your own fault. If you had only curtailed your impetuosity for a few minutes I am sure Celeste would have told you that you had no need to return at all. After Celeste and Vidal are married you can continue to stay on at the hotel as my guest.'

His face told her nothing of his thoughts and she blushed at her own imaginings. She had no doubt what being his guest would entail—nights spent in the luxury of his arms, their bodies intimately entwined, and in the daytime acting almost like strangers—in fact, all the things she feared. To let Cesare make love to her would only make it more difficult for her to give him up.

'That wouldn't be possible.' She held herself tautly, suppressing the desire to launch herself into his arms. Here and now wasn't the right time for that, and she hoped by the time they reached London she would have been able to put these thoughts out of her head— and her body, her traitorous body that softened against his in complete surrender, ignoring the logical dictates of her brain.

'You have nothing of importance to return to here,' he told her scathingly.

Suzanne's hackles rose. 'This may seem nothing to you, but it happens to be my home.'

'That is easily recognisable.'

'Are you being insulting?' she asked uncertainly.

'No, I am not,' he said patiently. 'The room is small, but it is completely you; bright and cheerful.'

'Oh.'

'Yes, oh. Now would you please get some of your things together so that we can be on our way. I do not want to arrive back too late.' He relaxed his long length in the only armchair in the room, watching her through shuttered eyes.

'Oh. Right.' She became flustered as he continued to watch her as she pulled out her suitcase from under the bed and began throwing things inside. She swore as a lace bra landed on the floor at his feet, picking it up and throwing it angrily into the case.

'Calm down, Suzanne,' Cesare broke into her angry mutterings. 'I am not in that much of a hurry.' He sat forward, taking the bra back out of the case. 'Very nice, but I prefer you without it. You do not need it, your body is young and beautiful.'

She snatched it out of his hand, burying it deep at the bottom of her case. 'I just have to go and say good-bye to Robert.'

'Is that necessary?'

She flushed. 'I believe so.'

'Very well.' He stood up in one fluid movement, picking up her securely locked suitcase. 'I will wait for you outside.'

Robert's door stood open, as had her own. Patsy was sprawled across the bed and Robert sat on the floor, but he stood up as she entered the room. 'What did he want?'

Suzanne explained the situation to him, not quite able to meet his searching eyes. 'He's waiting for me now,' she added.

'I see,' Robert said slowly. 'Do you have any idea when you'll be back?'

She shrugged. 'None at all, although I don't suppose

it will be long. The wedding's tomorrow, so I could possibly be back in the evening.'

Robert scoffed. 'I don't think so, love. In fact, I don't think we'll be seeing you back here at all.'

'What do you mean?' she asked sharply.

'I've seen the way he looks at you, Suzanne. I would say that at the first opportunity he'll have you in his bed—and not let you out for a week.'

'Robert!'

He laughed softly. 'Frightened? But a little excited too, I bet?'

'Don't be silly,' she evaded.

'You'd better go now.' He came forward and kissed her softly on the lips. 'Good luck, love. I hope you'll always be happy in your life.'

She looked at him searchingly. 'You make it sound like goodbye.'

He gently touched her cheek. 'I have a feeling that's exactly what it is.'

'You're wrong, Robert. You have to be.' She sounded almost desperate. Would she be able to leave Cesare again? It had been difficult enough the first time, she wasn't sure she would be able to do it again. She kissed Robert quickly and ran out of the room before she broke down. She had a feeling of dread, a feeling of inevitability, that he was right, that this was goodbye.

After a quick word with Mrs Holmes she went out of the house to find Cesare leaning casually against a sleek black Lamborghini, although he moved swiftly enough to open the door for her. He saw her comfortably seated before climbing into the driver's seat.

'Everything all right?' he queried softly.

'Fine.' She couldn't look at him, it would be her undoing. She was so much aware of him, of the closeness of his warm body, of his firm strong hands so sure on the wheel.

'You are very quiet,' he remarked about half an hour later.

'I have nothing to say,' she said primly.

Cesare laughed softly, a husky sound deep in his throat. 'Why are you sulking? You did not expect me to let you go so easily, did you? To meekly give up? But this is not my way, you must know that.'

'I—I—I don't know what you mean.'

'Yes, you do,' he contradicted gently. 'I want you, Suzanne, and I want you to say you will come to me.'

'I can't—I *won't* say that, because it wouldn't be true. I'm not suited to the type of life you described for us.'

'Have you considered seriously what I am offering you? A life free from any monetary problems—oh yes, Celeste has told me you both have no money, that the stay at the hotel was pure luxury for you. She has held nothing back, your hardship as a child, the way you have supported yourself the last few years. Does complete luxury not compare favourably with all that?'

'You must know it does, but I—I don't want to see you again once we reach the hotel!' she cried desperately.

'But we are not going to the hotel,' he told her calmly.

'We—we aren't? But—why aren't we?'

'Because I do not wish to go there. We are going to a house in Guildford. You know the town?'

'I've heard of it. But why are we going there?'

Cesare looked at her, raising one eyebrow mockingly. 'Why do you think?'

She turned in her seat to look at him. 'You—you can't mean it!'

'Oh, but I do.'

Another quick glance at his set face told her that he would not be moved by tears. But did she want to fight him any more? Didn't she want to give in, place her future in his hands, no matter what the outcome?

By the time they reached Guildford Suzanne was going alternately hot and cold, her legs felt shaky and she felt sure they wouldn't support her when she had to get out of the car. Cesare finally halted the car outside a well-lit detached house on the outskirts of the town, turning in his seat to look at her.

His arm moved along the back of her seat, his hand moved to caress her tense nape under her soft blonde waves. 'Will you come into the house with me, give yourself freely and with love, with no recriminations?'

Suzanne felt as if she were drowning in deep grey pools, was being tempted by eyes that compelled and cajoled at one and the same time. 'Yes,' she agreed huskily, feeling as if all this were happening in a dream. Was this really her casually agreeing to become Cesare's mistress?

He lifted one of her hands and kissed her fingers one by one, his eyes never leaving her face. 'Thank you, Suzanne,' was all he said.

Cesare let himself into the house, although at their entrance a woman of about forty-five came bustling into the reception area. 'Mr Cesare!' she greeted with a beaming smile in their general direction.

'You have prepared for us, Molly?' he asked after the preliminary greetings were over.

Again she smiled. 'Of course, sir. As it's so late would you like me to take you straight upstairs?'

'I think I can find my own way, thank you, Molly. We will want breakfast not later than eight-thirty—Vidal is marrying at eleven o'clock.'

'I know, sir. Isn't it exciting?'

'Yes, I suppose it is. Well, goodnight, Molly.'

'Goodnight, sir, madam.'

Suzanne mumbled some form of goodnight before slowly following Cesare as he mounted the stairs. 'Are you nervous, *cara*?' He turned to look at her.

Her eyes darkened. 'You must know I am. I don't

do this sort of thing every day of the week.'

'So I would hope.' He took her arm, leading her towards a closed door. 'Come, Suzanne, no one is going to hurt you, least of all me.' He opened the door and pushed her gently inside.

Suzanne's eyes opened wide with shock. This was certainly the expected bedroom—but it wasn't empty! Propped up in the huge double bed was an old lady of between seventy and eighty years of age, with hair that had once been as fair as the man's who stood at her side, now gone gracefully grey, but the face still remained beautiful, the grey eyes piercing.

Cesare moved forward, lifting one of the fragile white hands to kiss the fingertips. 'Grandmama,' he murmured, confirming Suzanne's half guessed at conclusion. He held out his other hand to Suzanne, and she walked forward as if in a dream to take it. 'Grandmama, I want you to meet Suzanne. She is to be the future Contessa Martino.'

CHAPTER TEN

'I know who she is, Cesare,' his grandmother said, her frail appearance belied by the strength of character in her voice. 'Now run along,' she dismissed. 'I'll send Suzanne along to her bedroom in a few minutes.'

To Suzanne's surprise the voice appeared to be as English as her own. But why surprise? This must be the mother of the English mother Cesare appeared to despise. Strangely enough her brain seemed to be functioning normally—strange, because she felt completely numb. Had Cesare really introduced her as his future wife? She felt sure he had, and yet it couldn't possibly be true.

'Run along, Cesare,' his grandmother repeated. 'I'm not going to eat the girl, just have a little chat with her.'

Cesare bent to kiss one powdered cheek. 'All right, Grandmama. But do not keep her long, it has been a long day for both of us.'

'Very well, Cesare,' she frowned at him impatiently. 'The sooner you leave the quicker Suzanne will be able to go to bed. I'll see you in the morning.'

Suzanne was still watching them as if in a dream. She felt Cesare bend and kiss her lips. He touched her cheek gently. 'We will talk tomorrow, Suzanne,' he promised.

His grandmother patted the bed for Suzanne to sit down, which she thankfully did, feeling almost as if she were falling down. 'I——' her voice came out in a squeak. 'I didn't know Cesare was bringing me here to meet you, Mrs——' she halted as she realised she didn't know her name. It wouldn't be the same as Cesare's, that was certain.

'You will call me Grandmama as Cesare and Vidal do.' The old lady searched Suzanne's face. 'You're very beautiful, my dear.'

Suzanne blushed. 'Thank you.'

'You appeared surprised when Cesare introduced you,' his grandmother said shrewdly. 'Is everything all right between the two of you?'

Suzanne gave an uncertain smile. 'I think so. What I mean is, I—I'm not sure.'

The older woman laughed. 'As usual Cesare has been arrogant. He hasn't even asked you to marry him, has he?'

'Well, no, but——'

'Isn't that just like Cesare?' his grandmother chuckled softly. 'You must try to understand that his arrogance is completely unrealised. I'm sure he'll get round to asking you some time. And your answer?'

'Answer?' Suzanne repeated vaguely.

'Will you be marrying my grandson?'

'If he asks me,' she nodded.

'Oh, he'll ask you, when he realises that he hasn't yet done so.' The old lady sat back with satisfaction. 'I met your stepmother today.'

'Celeste?'

'Yes. She and Vidal came to obtain my blessing on their marriage. I think they will be happy together. She will certainly keep Vidal on his toes.'

Suzanne felt herself beginning to relax. This woman wasn't half as frightening as she at first appeared. 'I think so too, although Cesare didn't feel too happy about them at first.'

'That was because of you. He believed you to be in love with Vidal, and if Vidal was what you needed to make you happy then he was going to make sure you got him. You would not have been happy with Vidal, Cesare will make you a much better husband.'

'I——'

'I know,' the old lady patted her hand reassuringly. 'You're rather bewildered by it all at the moment. Off you go to bed now, I just wanted to meet you and perhaps try to explain why Cesare is—well, as he is. You know about his mother?'

'Yes, he told me.'

'Mmm, Margaret was always irresponsible. That was probably my fault, I spoilt her terribly. Ah, well, that's water under the bridge now. He was very lonely as a child, I tried to be a mother to him, but—well, I wasn't used to little boys, Margaret was an only child. Then Marco, Cesare's father, married Vidal's mother. I moved out of the Palazzo, of course, finally thinking that Cesare had found someone to love him and be the mother he needed. And for a while it worked, then Maria died giving birth to Vidal. You can imagine the upheaval this caused to a child of five, to lose two women he loved so early in life.'

'Yes.' And Suzanne could. No wonder Cesare could be so aloof at times, almost as if he were shutting emotion out of his life. That was because that was exactly what he was doing.

'He had to grow up too soon,' his grandmother continued. 'He was never allowed to be a little boy as Vidal was. Marco left it up to me to bring up the two boys, and I'm afraid Vidal was always more easy to understand and love than the more complex Cesare. I'm only telling you all this to help you understand that Cesare will never be an easy person to live with.'

'I think I already know that.'

His grandmother smiled. 'Good. I'm glad we've had this little chat. Off you go now. Your room is two doors up on the right.'

It was a lovely room, overlooking the sizeable garden, but of course it was too dark to see any of it now. There was a huge double bed in the room, covered by a thick gold bedspread. The furniture was white and delicate, the carpet deep brown with a lovely thick pile that Suzanne sank her bare feet into. The adjoining bath-room was in matching brown and gold, and after a quick shower she climbed into the huge double bed, glad to relax her body, although her mind was too active for her to sleep.

She had entered this house this evening expecting to leave it after a night spent in Cesare's arms. But she had misjudged him. He had introduced her to his grandmother as his future contessa! Did he really mean to marry her? Did he love her? Hundreds of questions beseiged her and she knew she wouldn't sleep.

She turned sharply as the door handle slowly turned and a shadowy figure entered the room. 'It is only me, Suzanne,' Cesare said softly.

She sat up in the bed, her eyes searching the gloom. 'Cesare!' she breathed huskily.

He came to sit on the side of the bed, leaning for-ward to switch on the bedside lamp. He was clothed in grey trousers and a black silk shirt, and she felt her breath catch in her throat at the expression in his eyes. Had he come here to claim the admission she had made? Had he lied to his grandmother about making her his wife?

'Your eyes are very expressive, *cara*. I have come here for no other reason than to tell you I love you.'

'You—you love me?'

'So much.' He touched her parted lips. 'I did not come to Manchester today to bring you back for the wedding, I came because I could not believe you had dared to leave without saying goodbye to me.'

'I dared.'

'I know that,' his mouth tightened angrily. 'But why did you dare?'

'You must know why.' She looked away.

'Because of what I said to you. I was wrong to do that to you. I was punishing you, I suppose.' He stood up to walk up and down the room. 'Even tonight, on the way here, I could not stop hurting you, testing you.' He stopped his prowling to look at her. 'I am sorry for that, but it did tell me what I wanted to know.'

'And what was that?' Suzanne was almost afraid to put the question to him, fearing the answer and that he might still be testing her.

'You love me too,' a smile lit his features. 'I want to hear you say it, Suzanne. Tell me. Please.'

She looked away. 'I can't—I can't tell you anything. I—I don't trust you. You could be testing me again just to taunt me.'

A look of pain crossed his face. 'Oh, God, what have I done to you!' He came back to sit on the bed, grasping her arms to pull her roughly against him. 'I love you, Suzanne. I love you! I have not meant to hurt you, I love you too much to ever want to do that again.'

'Then why did you do it?' It was an anguished cry.

'Because I have never learned trust, I realise that now. I need proof all the time. You see, even now I cannot be sure you love me. You have not said it, but I have to tell you of my own feelings anyway. It no longer matters that you love me in return. I went back to Venice in the hope of forgetting you, I threw myself back into my work and a hectic social life. After a week I was ready to come back, after two weeks I was almost going insane.'

Suzanne put a hand to stop his words. 'No more, Cesare. You don't have to say any more.'

He removed her hand, turning away. 'I want to. I want you to know how badly I felt when I came back to find you in Robert Thompson's arms, how it made me cruel with you. But even then I could not leave you alone, I had to insult you by asking you to be my mistress. I was in the wrong earlier,' his face was haggard. 'I should not have introduced you to my grandmother as my future wife. Why should you want to marry me?

I've never been kind to you, have never acted in a way to evoke your softer feelings towards me.'

'Please, Cesare, stop this self-torture!' she begged, jumping out of the bed and running into his arms. 'I love you, I want you, I need you. If you really want to marry me I'll willingly say yes. Do you want to marry me?'

'So much, it hurts,' he groaned.

'Oh, Cesare!' She stood on tiptoe to part his lips with her own. Darling Cesare, usually so arrogant and superior, now as vulnerable as herself when it came to falling in love.

Her surrender was all he needed to mould her against him with a savagery that hurt her, but it was a pain she would willingly stand for the rest of her life. He crushed her to him until she found it almost impossible to breathe, plundering her mouth until she felt breathless, her head spinning.

He cradled each side of her face, his smile for her alone. 'Oh, my darling, you have made me so happy.' He searched her face. 'You are sure about this? I will not let you go once I have you.'

She laughed huskily, tears of happiness slipping slowly down her cheeks. 'I just want to be with you—always.'

Cesare strained her to him again. 'And so you shall be,' he promised huskily. 'Oh, *cara*, tell me again that you love me.'

'I love you, I love you, I love you!' she cried happily.

He kissed her temple, his hands moving expertly over her body. 'I will want to hear it every minute of the day,' he warned.

'Don't worry,' she laughed unsteadily. 'You probably will. I can't seem to stop saying it now I've started.'

He looked down at her scantily clad body. 'You must get back into bed, my darling. You are hardly dressed to receive visitors.'

She clung to him. 'You, I am. Don't go, Cesare. Don't leave me.'

A nerve pulsed erratically at his jawbone. 'I have to, Suzanne. I only came in here to tell you of my feelings for you. I certainly could not sleep until I had done so, and I doubt if you could also.'

'I couldn't,' she admitted. 'I was totally confused. Your grandmother didn't seem at all surprised when you called me—when you said I was——'

'When I said you were going to be my wife,' he finished firmly. 'Grandmama was not surprised because I had already told her all about you,' he smiled wryly. 'I seem to have told her of nothing else since I first met you.'

Her eyes widened. 'Since you first met me? But you didn't like me.'

'But I did, Suzanne. Too much, in fact. I could almost have resorted to violence when I saw how attracted to Vidal you were. But I knew that if I did that I would only make you dislike me more, and you did dislike me, did you not?'

She nodded almost guiltily. 'I'm afraid so.'

He kissed her gently on her parted lips. 'It is all right, cara. You had every reason to feel like that.' He heaved a deep sigh. 'I was a brute with you. But I did not try to get you to love me to prevent you going out with Vidal, he did not enter into my thoughts at all. I wanted you for myself, for no other reason. I was not fair in my dealings with you at all, I could not allow you to be alone with him even for a few minutes. Even that day we took you both sightseeing, I made sure you spent more time with me than with Vidal.'

'You don't mind about their marriage now?'

'I only minded in the first place for your sake. Mario Danieli's daughter would never have been able to keep Vidal at her side, I realise that now.'

'And there will be no scandal?' she asked anxiously.

'No. I am afraid I rather exaggerated the possibility of Vidal marrying Carla. It was discussed once between Mario and myself, but Vidal has shown his aversion to such an arrangement from the first. I could not force the issue because I myself was never willing to accept an arranged marriage for myself. I think Vidal and Celeste deserve each other.'

'Your grandmother said something along the same lines.' Suzanne fidgeted awkwardly with one of the buttons on his shirt. 'Cesare, you—you said——'

'Do not be shy, my love. I have no secrets from you.'

'Your fiancée,' she said in a rush. 'You said she died?'

'If you get back into bed I will tell you about Estella.' She did as he asked, scrambling back under the covers. 'That is better,' he said tightly. 'This way I cannot feel your delightful body so close against me. We have to marry soon, Suzanne. I love you too much to wait too long. You have already witnessed that I do not have too much control where you are concerned.'

She blushed prettily. 'And Estella?'

He smiled at her. 'I have not forgotten Estella. I became betrothed to her when I was only eighteen and she was seventeen. The marriage was not to take place until I reached twenty-one and was considered adult enough to marry. The betrothal was not my idea, but my father was determined to see me safely married with a family of my own to care for. Perhaps he thought I had some of my mother's flightiness, I do not know, but he was not the sort of man you argued with. And in his way he was right, but unfortunately he died when I was only twenty.'

'I know,' she put in softly. 'Vidal told me.'

'Mm,' he frowned disapprovingly at the mention of his brother and she realised that even now he could be jealous of him. She doubted he would get over his uncertainty until they had been married some time and he could feel sure of her love for him. Married! Her heart still leapt at the thought of it. She longed with every part of her to be his wife.

'And?' she prompted.

'And I had to become the Conte earlier than expected. The marriage was delayed, and before it could take place at a later date Estella had died. She was always delicate as a child, but a chance cold turned to pneumonia. There was nothing to be done. If she had lived we would have married, I could not have let her down even though I did not love her. But she did die, and I could not bring myself to enter into another arrangement of that kind.'

Her hands slid over his shoulders to bring his head down so that her lips might touch his. 'I'm glad you didn't. I might just have been tempted to enter into that affair with a married man you keep accusing me of having. Only you would have been the married man.'

He frowned. 'Celeste has a vitriolic tongue, she ought to be beaten for telling me such a lie. Vidal will have a hard time controlling her,' this caused him some amusement. Then his face sobered. 'You are sure you want to marry a man so much older than you? Eighteen years are not to be taken lightly.'

'I love you. I want to marry you,' she told him firmly.

'Then that is all that matters.' His head lowered to claim her lips.

Cesare stirred next to her in the huge double bed and she stretched lazily, her arms above her head. For the past fifteen minutes she had been watching the play of emotions across her husband's face. She had done the same thing every day of their year of marriage, cherishing these precious few minutes of absolute peace before the pressures of the day would take Cesare away from her.

A three-month honeymoon of extensive travelling

about Europe had not prepared her for the time when Cesare would shut himself off in the business part of the Palazzo from ten o'clock in the morning sometimes until quite late at night. But he always had time for her, she could never accuse him of neglecting her. He had taken her to all the beautiful haunts of Venice he had once promised her. Nevertheless, these few minutes together in the morning were important to her, a time when they could be completely alone.

It hadn't been easy for her to fit into the role of the Contessa Martino, having no training for such a position, but Cesare had been a tremendous help to her, never scolding and standing by her if occasionally she happened to make a mistake. She smiled to herself. During the first few months at home after their honeymoon she had made plenty; on one more memorable occasion she had put one of Cesare's ageing aunts next to a nephew she simply couldn't stand. She and Cesare had laughed about it afterwards, but it had been rather embarrassing at the time, with the aged aunt demanding to be moved immediately. Luckily enough Cesare had smoothed things over and the dinner party had turned out to be a big success.

He opened his sleepy grey eyes now, reaching up to pull her down to him. He nuzzled into her neck. 'Good morning, *cara mia*. What are you thinking so earnestly about?'

She squirmed with pleasure as his lips travelled down her neck and over her bare shoulders. 'I was thinking of our life together,' she admitted.

'Were they good thoughts?' he murmured from the depths of her creamy throat.

She smiled. 'Oh, very good.'

He leant on his elbow looking down at her. 'I am glad.'

'How could they be anything else?' She pulled him down to her, raining fevered kisses over his face. 'I love you, Cesare. I want you to love me.'

'And what of the maid bringing up our morning coffee?' he teased lightly.

'She won't come until you ring for her—that one time she did taught her never to do it again. You were in a foul temper for the rest of the day,' Suzanne laughed huskily.

'She had no right to interrupt us like that.' His eyes darkened with passion. 'And I will personally murder her if she does so now.' His lips touched hers and Suzanne knew herself lost. . . .

Hours later, her head resting on Cesare's bare chest, she sighed contentedly. 'I suppose we'll have to get out of bed soon, Cesare. Celeste and Vidal will be arriving soon.'

'Oh God, yes! I had forgotten. And you have kept me here when I should be preparing myself to receive them,' he frowned. 'When do they arrive?'

'In about two hours' time, just after lunch, Celeste said. And did I really keep you here?'

'No, you witch, I could not leave you. Your body torments me. I find myself thinking of you at the most inopportune moments, in the middle of a business meeting, when we have people to dinner. It can be most embarrassing at times.'

'I'm sorry,' she said demurely, looking at him between lowered lashes.

Cesare threw back the bedclothes, getting reluctantly out of the bed. 'I could stay here and make love to you all day, but I will not let you tempt me. Get yourself dressed, baggage, we must prepare to greet our guests.'

'Are you pleased about their baby?' she asked casually, watching closely for his reaction. There was none.

'Of course I am,' he put on a navy silk bathrobe. 'And Vidal is as excited as a young boy.'

Suzanne continued to watch his face. 'We could——' she took a deep breath and started again. 'We could have a baby. Would you like that?' She waited breathlessly for his answer.

'We have discussed this before, Suzanne,' he said stiffly. We have plenty of time to have a family, so I do not see the point of discussing it. I am in no hurry.'

'But, Cesare——'

'We have plenty of time, Suzanne,' he repeated hardly, opening the door to their bathroom and closing it firmly behind him.

She made an effort to act naturally in front of Celeste and Vidal, but it was proving quite a strain and she felt relieved when at last Cesare and Vidal disappeared into the office to discuss a business deal.

'Well,' Celeste sat back more comfortably in the ornate chair. 'Now perhaps you'll tell me what's wrong with you?'

'Wrong with me?' Suzanne repeated shrilly. 'Why should there be anything wrong with me?'

'Because I know you, Suzanne. Perhaps not as well as I should, but better than you give me credit for.'

Suzanne attempted a light laugh. 'You're becoming quite maternal, Celeste. I must say you're positively blooming.'

'Vidal and I are very happy about the baby. But you haven't answered my question.'

Suzanne looked away. 'There's nothing wrong with me. Cesare and I are very happy together.'

'I know that. But at certain times you have shadows in your eyes. Tell me what's wrong, Suzanne. I'm trying to help you,' Celeste said softly.

'You wouldn't understand, Celeste.' Suzanne fidgeted nervously with the silk covering on the chair.

'Then there is something wrong. Is it the baby?'

Suzanne looked up sharply. 'Don't be silly! Cesare is very pleased for both of you.'

'I don't mean my baby, I mean yours.'

'Mine?' Suzanne evaded. 'But I'm not—— Yes, I am! I'm having a baby!'

Celeste smiled. 'I thought that was it. I could see there was something different about you. What did Cesare say when you told him?'

'I—I haven't told him. He refuses to talk about it.'

'How can he, when you haven't even told him?'

'He refuses to discuss having a family at all. I just don't know what to do. How can I tell him!'

'Well, he's going to know in a couple of months' time anyway—you can't hide something like having a baby.'

'But he doesn't want a family!'

Celeste frowned. 'It's a bit late to realise that now. Anyway, are you sure he feels that way?'

'I told you, he won't even talk about it.'

Celeste licked her lips. 'Actually, Suzanne, this was discussed when Cesare talked to me about marrying you. He seemed to consider twenty-four, twenty-five, was quite young enough for you to become a mother. I was inclined to agree with him.'

'You *discussed* it? But why?' Suzanne demanded.

Celeste shrugged. 'Cesare felt it necessary. He probably thinks you're offering to have a baby because you feel it's your duty, and that's the one thing he doesn't want you to feel. His own mother had him out of duty, and you know how that marriage ended.'

'But I want this baby. I want *his* baby!'

'Then I suggest you tell him that. But wait until you're completely alone and can be sure you won't be interrupted, preferably tonight when you go to bed. I'm sure you'll be proved wrong, I'm sure Cesare would like a child very much.'

'I hope you're right,' Suzanne sighed.

She took longer over her shower that evening, longing to tell Cesare about their baby and yet dreading perhaps spoiling the wonderful relationship they already had. They loved each other, of that she had no doubt, but a baby that wasn't wanted completely by both of them could ruin everything. But Celeste was right, she couldn't keep quiet for much longer. Already she was having to linger in bed until Cesare had gone down to breakfast, earning herself much teasing from Cesare, calling her lazybones and other names like that. It wasn't that she was lazy at all, it was just that immediately she stepped out of bed nausea overtook her and she had to rush to the bathroom.

Cesare poked his head around the bathroom door as she stood drying herself, his eyes darkening at her nakedness. 'Are you not coming to bed, Suzanne?'

'Oh yes—yes. I—I won't be a moment.' She finished drying herself and donned her sheer blue cotton night-dress before padding into the bedroom. She looked down guiltily. 'Cesare, I—I have something I want to talk to you about.'

He patted the vacant half of the bed beside him. 'Come to bed, *cara*, we can talk better in each other's arms.'

She was tempted, but slowly shook her head. She couldn't think straight when in his arms. 'No, I—I can tell you better from over here.'

Cesare leant back against the velvet headboard, his arms folded across his bare chest. 'That sounds ominous. What have you done? Spent all your allowance?'

'You know my allowance is far too much for me to spend it all! I hardly go anywhere where I can spend money anyway.'

'Is that what is wrong with you, you wish to go out more? You have only to say, Suzanne, you know I will take you wherever——'

'Will you be quiet, Cesare!' she cut in, her voice rising in her agitation. 'I don't want to talk to you about that at all. I—I'm going to have a baby! No——' she couldn't look at him, 'I don't want you to say anything. I love you, Cesare, I love you very much. And I want this baby. I know it's too soon, I know you don't want a child yet, but it wasn't my fault!' To her horror she burst into tears. 'It wasn't my fault,' she repeated brokenly.

Cesare burst into a torrent of his own language, something he didn't do very often in her company. Oh God, he was angry! What could she do? She heard him close behind her and felt herself pulled back against the hardness of his body, his face buried in her throat as his hands spread possessively across her still flat stomach.

'You carry my child,' he said in a voice of wonder. 'A child made from our love.'

Her eyes widened at the gentleness of his voice. 'You —you aren't angry?'

He spun her round to face him, his face lit by the most tender smile she had ever seen. 'Angry?' he looked puzzled. 'Why should I be angry?'

'I thought you would be.' Relief began to enter her body and she felt almost faint. 'I—— You never seemed to want to talk about it. I thought—I thought perhaps —because of your mother you didn't trust me to have your child, that you didn't want me to have a child and then desert you.'

Cesare led her over to the bed and sat her down. 'You must take things easy now, I shall have to be as protective over you as Vidal is with Celeste. I think I will enjoy spoiling you a little more.'

'But, Cesare——'

'Hush, *cara*,' he tucked her beneath the covers. 'You must not distress yourself any more. Your imagination has been working overtime these last few weeks. To imagine I do not want you to have my child! I admit I did not want it to happen just yet, but that was for your sake, not mine. You married young, I did not want you to become a mother until you were ready for it.

But it had nothing to do with the way my mother acted, you are nothing like my mother.' He switched out the light and she felt the bed give on his side as he climbed in beside her, pulling her gently into the circle of his arms. 'I want this baby too,' he kissed her softly. 'And if you're happy about it being now then it is not too soon, it is just right. But I have to disagree with you about it not being your fault. I consider it solely your fault.'

'You—you do?'

'Mmm,' his body hardened against her. 'You tempt me until I cannot think straight, drive me to distraction at the most inconvenient times, until I can think of nothing but making love to you. Like now.'

'Oh, Cesare!' she smiled at him tremulously.

'Come, Suzanne, can you not show me how much you love me, before our child makes it impossible for you to do so?'

She touched him with feather-light fingertips. 'We have months before that happens.'

She saw him grin in the darkness. 'I know that, but I intend to take full advantage of the opportunities left to me. Now, kiss me.'

'Yes, Cesare.' And she proceeded to do so.

What readers say about Harlequin Romances

"Your books turn my...life into something quite exciting."
B.M.,* Baldwin Park, California

"I have never read a Harlequin that I did not like. They are all wonderful books."
M.H., Hatboro, Pennsylvania

"Harlequin books have afforded me more pleasure than I ever anticipated."
C.S.P., Riverdale, Georgia

"I have one complaint...there are never enough Harlequins."
N.S., Horace, North Dakota

*Names available on request

Remember when a good love story made you feel like holding hands?

The wonder of love is timeless.
Once discovered, love remains,
despite the passage of time.
Harlequin brings you stories of
true love, about women the
world over – women like you.

*Harlequin Romances
with the
Harlequin magic...*

Recapture the sparkle of first
love...relive the joy of true
romance...enjoy these stories
of love today.

Six new novels every month –
wherever paperbacks
are sold.

3 GREAT NOVELS

Harlequin brings you a book to cherish ...

three stories of
love and romance
by one of your
favorite
Harlequin authors ...

JOY
ROMANCE
LOVE

Harlequin Omnibus
THREE love stories in ONE beautiful volume

The joys of being in love...
the wonder of romance...
the happiness that true love brings...

Now yours in the HARLEQUIN OMNIBUS edition every month wherever paperbacks are sold.

NEW FROM HARLEQUIN

YOUR 1980 ROMANCE HOROSCOPE!

Harlequin Reader Service

In U.S.A.
M.P.O. Box 707
Niagara Falls, NY 14302

In Canada
649 Ontario Street
Stratford, Ontario, N5A 6W2

Please send me the following Harlequin Romance Horoscope
volumes. I am enclosing a check or money order of $1.75 for each
volume ordered, plus 40¢ to cover postage and handling.

☐ Aries
(Mar. 21-Apr. 20)

☐ Taurus
(Apr 21-May 22)

☐ Gemini
(May 23-June 21)

☐ Cancer
(June 22-July 22)

☐ Leo
(July 23-Aug. 22)

☐ Virgo
(Aug. 23-Sept. 22)

☐ Libra
(Sept. 23-Oct. 22)

☐ Scorpio
(Oct. 23-Nov. 21)

☐ Sagittarius
(Nov. 22-Dec. 22)

☐ Capricorn
(Dec. 23-Jan. 20)

☐ Aquarius
(Jan. 21-Feb. 19)

☐ Pisces
(Feb. 20-Mar 20)

Number of volumes checked @ $1.75 each $_____

N.Y. and N.J. residents add appropriate sales tax $_____

Postage and handling $_____.40

                                            TOTAL: $_____

I am enclosing a grand total of $_____

NAME_____

ADDRESS_____

STATE/PROV._____ ZIP/POSTAL CODE_____

PRS 323